Sign up for our newsletter to hear
about new and upcoming releases.

www.ylva-publishing.com

OTHER BOOKS BY A.L. BROOKS

Up on the Roof
Miles Apart
Dark Horse
The Club

ONE WAY
OR ANOTHER

A. L. BROOKS

ACKNOWLEDGEMENTS

Thank you, Ylva, for letting me play with the Window Shopping series—it's such a fun premise to tackle!

A big shout-out to my editor, Alissa, who taught me a whole heap of stuff about not repeating the obvious and trusting your readers, and to Sheena for excellent proofing and spotting of awkward little sentences that needed a good tweak!

My beta readers were incredibly patient with all the rewrites this one underwent, dropping everything to read the latest version and give me essential feedback, so massive thanks go to Katja and Erin.

Glendon, the cover is wonderful—thank you for bringing to life exactly what I had imagined.

Andrea Bramhall continues to be an important mentor, sounding board, and project manager who is always there when I need to talk, and for that, she gets a big hug the next time I see her.

Tanja, my partner—your support means the absolute world to me, and being a writer is a vastly more wonderful occupation with you by my side. Thank you, my love.

DEDICATION

In memory of Nellie Bewley

CHAPTER 1

THE SUN REFLECTED OFF THE window, obscuring the view of the shop inside. Still, Bethany was hyperaware of the products on display. She shuffled her feet and coughed but didn't move towards the door. In the window, she caught the reflection of another woman's easy smile, as if she frequented sex-toy stores all the time.

Even in the distorted reflection, the woman was incredibly attractive. Maybe two inches taller than Bethany's five foot eight, she had dark hair cut in a pixie style that suited her high cheekbones and elegant jawline. She was dressed in a dark-coloured trouser suit with a jacket that dipped in at her waist and flared out slightly over her hips. It was a sophisticated look, and the woman carried it off with style. Her smile was wide, and although Bethany was tempted to return it, her nerves over the adventure she was about to undertake prevented her lips from moving.

A soft breeze lifted Bethany's hair and brought her back to herself. Her eyes focused on the window before her, and the tantalising array of products on sale. She could barely believe she was here, and although her heart was thumping in her chest at the prospect of climbing those stairs and walking through that door, at the same time a thrill was coursing through her. Shopping online would have been far easier, and less nerve-wracking, but Bethany had always known it would come to this for this particular purchase. Seeing—and touching—would be essential to make the correct choice.

Vibrator. Even the word sent a shiver of anticipated pleasure skittering down her spine to settle somewhere deep between her legs. In this day and age, buying a vibrator was commonplace for many women—but not

Bethany. She'd made the decision back in college to focus on her studies and her ambition to become a teacher, and as a result, sex and relationships had fallen by the wayside, easily discarded in the pursuit of a higher goal. Now that the goal had been obtained, and she was five years into her teaching career, old urges—and some new ones that she really wasn't sure what to do with—had surfaced, and were in desperate need of attention.

So, here she was, standing outside a sex shop in the heart of London, the thirty-minute Tube journey having done nothing to calm her nervous excitement. Her palms were damp, and she wiped them on the pleats of the light summer dress she wore. She adjusted her handbag on her shoulder, and pushed a few wayward strands of hair back behind the arms of her glasses.

"They have lots more inside, you know."

She jumped.

"God, I'm so sorry. I thought you heard me approach."

The voice was deeper than her own, with a hint of huskiness about it that caused a disconcerting fluttering sensation across the back of Bethany's neck. She turned her head, meeting the gaze of the tall woman in the suit, who was now smiling widely at her.

Embarrassment at reacting so twitchily made the manners Bethany's mother had instilled in her from a young age flee, and she snapped out her next words before she could contain herself.

"Well, obviously, I didn't."

"Wow," the woman said, frowning as she tilted her head. "I do believe I apologised, but if that's not good enough for you…"

A throat cleared beside them and a woman's voice said, "Miss Keane?"

Bethany turned, her face still set in a scowl, to find the mother of one of her pupils standing a couple of feet away. Lucinda Marchbanks. Of course, it would have to be—Mrs Marchbanks' ideas about the education of her little darling often clashed with Bethany's, and many a parents' evening had been more of heated debate than a report on little Michael's progress.

"Mrs Marchbanks," Bethany murmured. "Hello."

"How funny that I should bump into you this evening. Michael came home from school today rather upset. Apparently you sent him to the corner this morning?"

Stifling a groan, and ignoring the soft chuckle behind her—was that woman still there?—Bethany inhaled deeply.

"Yes, that's right, I did. He pinched Camilla."

To her credit, Lucinda Marchbanks relaxed her posture somewhat, although her voice still held a huff as she said, "Well, he's a boisterous child. I'm sure he didn't mean anything by it."

The dark-haired woman snorted, and Bethany rounded on her.

"Do you mind? This doesn't concern you."

The woman grinned, held up her hands and backed away, but did not, much to Bethany's annoyance, actually disappear. Instead, she made a show of crossing her arms and leaning casually against the sex-shop window.

The action, of course, made Lucinda Marchbanks look her way, and Bethany's cheeks burned as Lucinda's eyes widened and her eyebrows shot up her forehead. She pointed at the shop before turning her gaze back on Bethany.

"Are you…? Is this…?" Lucinda's voice was a squeak.

None of your damn business, yes. "Oh, er, no. I was…I was just passing." She'd wanted to be brave, and say 'yes, I am intending to shop here,' but the glare of Lucinda's green eyes wilted her courage. It probably was for the best—the last thing she needed was Lucinda Marchbanks spreading God knows what about her to the other parents.

There was another soft chuckle behind her, which thankfully didn't seem to carry to Lucinda's ears. Bethany gritted her teeth and resisted the impulse to turn round and tell the woman to get lost. "Look, Lucinda, perhaps we can talk another time. I don't think standing in the street is—"

Lucinda straightened to her full height, an intimidating five foot ten, and glared down at Bethany. "Michael is a good boy, with bags of energy. I do think you need to take that into account during your lessons."

"Mrs Marchbanks, I can certainly do that, but not to the detriment of Michael's classmates. Now, can I suggest that we meet at the school about this if you still have concerns?"

"Yeah, you tell her," whispered the dark-haired woman, only this time it appeared that Lucinda Marchbanks heard her. Bethany cringed as Lucinda looked past her, and turned to see the woman still leaning on the front of the shop.

3

"Do you mind? This is a private conversation." Lucinda's tone was haughty.

"Not if you're having it in the middle of the street it isn't." The woman grinned, but there was fire in her eyes.

Bethany wanted to crawl away from the situation, but knew she was trapped.

"Lucinda," she said, her tone placating, "why don't you and I talk on Monday, hm? When you come to collect Michael."

"Well," Lucinda huffed, still glaring at the other woman. "I suppose we can do that." She turned back to Bethany, eyes blazing, and Bethany took an involuntary step backwards. "Have a good evening," Lucinda said, flicking a glance between Bethany and the stranger that made her feel as if she were under a microscope.

Lucinda Marchbanks spun on her heel and strode off up the street, and Bethany's heart rate gradually started to slow.

"Well, thank God she's gone."

Bethany rounded on the woman, her irritation soaring. "Just who the hell do you think you are?" she snapped.

The woman—*how dare she?*—grinned.

"Oh, come on. Who the hell did she think she was?" she said, uncrossing her arms and walking a couple of paces nearer. "Accosting you in the street with something that was, quite frankly, a load of shit."

"Do we know each other?"

The woman frowned slightly. "Well, no, but—"

"Then what gives you the right to butt into my conversation—my business?"

The woman smiled that infuriating, cheeky grin again. "Hey, she was giving you a hard time, and I do so hate to see a damsel in distress."

"You cannot be serious." Bethany stared at her. *What planet was this woman from?* "I don't need you fighting my battles for me. I can look after myself, thank you very much."

"Hey, come on. You can't blame a girl for trying."

The woman was still smiling, and Bethany's heart was back to pounding out its stressed rhythm. How could someone so attractive on the outside be so...shallow on the inside?

"Look, this conversation is over. Please don't talk to me again."

Bethany spun round, and as she did so her handbag slipped down her arm and, before she could grab it, fell to the pavement. It burst open on contact, and to her mortification, the entire contents scattered. Her face flushed, and she knelt to start scooping everything up.

"Here, let me help," the woman said, sitting on her haunches next to Bethany.

"No, thank you." Bethany's tone was clipped, her hands scrabbling to gather all of her possessions as quickly as possible.

"Look, I'm sorry. I guess I did come across a bit strong just now." The woman's tone had completely changed—gone was the cockiness, the cheekiness. Now there was nothing but sincerity, and Bethany couldn't help but turn to look at her.

The woman really was stunning, especially up close. Her deep brown eyes were framed with lush eyelashes, and her skin was lightly tanned, which only emphasised her extraordinary cheekbones. Her lips were full and naturally deep pink. Bethany realised she was staring again, and dragged her gaze away.

"Yes, well. You did," Bethany replied, concentrating on cramming everything back into her handbag.

"It's just, well, you seemed nervous when you first looked in the window, and then that woman was just being a bitch to you and..."

Bethany risked another glance at the woman, who was still crouched down at her level. Her confusion escalated; there was nothing but concern and...tenderness etched on the stranger's face.

"I-I was... Nervous," she admitted, and blushed.

The woman nodded slowly. She pointed at the remnants of Bethany's handbag still scattered at their feet. "Can I help?"

"I-I... Thank you. Yes." Bethany cringed as her voice croaked, and looked away again, grateful for a few moments not to look into that beautiful face and feel like a stuttering teenager.

They gathered the remaining escapees—including, to yet more mortification, the small box of tampons Bethany kept in the inner pocket—then both stood.

"Thank you," Bethany whispered, clutching her bag to her abdomen.

The woman dipped her head. "You're welcome." She glanced up at the shop window. "Look, I'm a regular here. It's a very welcoming place, you know. In case you were worried."

Her expression was soft and understanding, and Bethany managed a weak smile, despite everything that had gone before.

"Th-thanks. That's good to know."

The woman smiled again. "See you inside."

And with that, she turned and walked to the two steps that led to the shop door. Bethany watched those long legs as they ascended, then snapped her gaze away as she realised it was journeying up the legs to the perfectly curved bottom perched at the top.

Ogling women was not something Bethany made a habit of. While comfortable in her sexuality since she'd had her first—and only—girlfriend in college, she liked to think of herself as somewhat more highbrow than someone who lasciviously stared at random women she bumped into outside a sex shop. Even if that sex shop was women-run and made a specific point of advertising itself as a safe space for any non-straight customers.

Flustered, Bethany pressed a palm to her warm cheek.

For goodness sakes, calm down. You came here for one purpose, so take a deep breath and get on with it.

Straightening her spine, she sucked in two extended lungfuls of air, exhaling slowly on each one. She fixed the strap on the handbag, hoisted it onto her shoulder, and then, before she could overthink it any further, she stepped to her left, climbed the two steps, and walked through the door.

CHAPTER 2

SARAH WOULDN'T NORMALLY STOP OUTSIDE the shop before entering and launch herself at a random woman hovering by the window, but the woman's understated beauty had stopped her in her tracks.

The woman—Miss Keane, she thought she'd heard that uptight cow call her—had the cute, nerdy look down pat. Her floral print summer dress was shades of pink and grey, and practical yet surprisingly attractive sandals adorned her feet, with painted pink toenails peeping through at the ends. Her body, as far as Sarah could tell with one extended look, was slim and full in the chest. She had hair of a nondescript brown colour that some would probably call mousey, and it fell in soft waves to just past her ears. But it was the glasses that had Sarah smiling—full on, thick-framed but stylishly modern glasses that reminded her of Nomi in *Sense8*.

Sarah was a huge sucker for nerdy glasses—as well as for a pretty woman looking lost and forlorn.

And when their eyes met in the window, the smile split Sarah's face before she'd even thought about it. Miss Keane looking rapidly away only made Sarah smile more, and wonder if today she would get to pick up more than a bottle of lube in the shop.

The incident with that stupid parent and the handbag nearly ruined things, but she was confident that she rescued the situation with her final words. And they were, after all, both heading into the shop, so Sarah had plenty of time to lay on more of the charm. Although, she begrudgingly had to admit, perhaps not as full on as she'd attempted initially. She'd misread Miss Keane, and she wouldn't make that mistake again; cute and nerdy did not mean weak and feeble. Lesson learned.

She smiled. She could imagine what Aunt Evelyn would have to say about this. And Jonathan too. As much as she loved them, their self-appointed roles as her lifestyle advisors had been grating on her nerves lately.

Squaring her shoulders—and shoving all thoughts of exactly what the pair of them would say into the far recesses of her mind—she strode into the shop.

Mira, all long blonde hair and curves, greeted her from behind the counter. "Sarah! Long time, no see."

Sarah remembered her first visit to the shop, maybe four years ago, and being more than a little overwhelmed by Mira's obvious enthusiasm for her job. There was welcoming, and there was "Oh my God, will you please get out of my face you over-perky chipmunk". Mira skirted a fine line between the two.

Still, it wasn't every shop you frequented where they bothered to find out your name *and* offered you a pretty good coffee thirty seconds after you walked through the door, so she couldn't complain.

"Espresso?" Mira asked, already walking towards the small Nespresso machine by the side window.

"You read my mind." Sarah wandered over to meet her at the machine, taking the proffered cup once the hot fluid had trickled its way to completion.

"How's life?"

Sarah blew on the coffee before taking a sip. "Not bad. Overworked, as usual."

Mira returned to the counter. "What are you in here for today?"

"Oh, just some lube. But I'll check out the books too."

And Miss Keane, who's just stepped in the door.

"Cool. Shout if you need anything, or another coffee."

Sarah raised a hand in acknowledgement, her quota of Mira time now filled, and leaned against the window sill next to the coffee machine. Her gaze landed on the nervous-looking Miss Keane, who was now the focus of Mira's attention. Poor thing looked like a rabbit caught in the headlights.

Sarah studied her over the rim of her coffee cup as she sipped. What was a mouse of a woman like her doing in a shop like this? Although, to be fair, this shop was probably the most welcoming you'd find—certainly in London—if you were in any way interested in adding something non-vanilla to your sex life. She swallowed. Non-vanilla was certainly something she craved, deep down, but not something she'd ever found the courage to really explore. Maybe she and the mouse-like Miss Keane were more alike than she'd first thought.

I wonder what you're after, cute thing. And I wonder if I could help you with that.

Sarah shook her head and winced. She sounded like a line from a bad porn movie. And also like she was falling straight into her usual *modus operandi*—seeking out the women who were least likely to give her what she truly desired.

She returned the empty cup to the tray holding the Nespresso machine and wandered across the shop to the bookshelf. The distraction of a range of lesbian erotic titles was probably just what she needed right now.

Or not, she thought, as her gaze once again, and almost against her will, returned to the cute woman she'd met outside.

For all that Miss Keane stirred Sarah's libido—to be honest, many women did—somehow another feeling swept over Sarah when she looked at her, and it was the same feeling that had made her step in with that vile Mrs Marchbanks.

Tenderness.

Sarah tore her gaze away from the woman and forced herself to look at the titles on the erotica shelf even as she rolled her eyes at herself. *Tenderness? Her? Sarah Connolly didn't know what the word meant.*

Except, she did, when she glanced back at Miss Keane, strolling around the shop, eyes wide behind her glasses. God, she was cute, and that weird feeling swamped Sarah again. That feeling like she wanted to protect her even as she pushed her up against the wall and kissed her senseless.

Okay, okay, this is getting ridiculous. Get a bloody grip on yourself.

This time she not only looked away from the woman, but physically turned so that she couldn't even see her out of the corner of her eye.

Yes, that was much better. Wasn't it?

"Hello there. Welcome!" the sales assistant called out as Bethany stepped through the door.

"Hello," Bethany squeaked, alarmed at the gusto with which she'd been greeted. *What was that woman on?*

"Would you like a tea or coffee?"

Bethany startled. *A hot drink? Now? Don't be absurd.*

"No, I'm...fine. Thank you."

"Okay! Feel free to browse, or ask any questions you may have."

"I-I will. Thank you."

Bethany managed a smile, remembering that her manners had already let her down once and determined not to slack again.

The assistant returned the smile—actually, she beamed—before continuing with her task. Bethany stared—were those dildo harnesses the woman was attaching to small hangers? They were in multiple colours and designs, and the thought of their purpose brought a quick flush to Bethany's cheeks. Images of what she'd like to do with a woman while wearing one of those threatened to blow a fuse somewhere in the back of her brain.

As much as she'd anticipated this—that this shop would tap into all her deepest fantasies—the reality was even more electric than she'd imagined. Her skin was actually buzzing simply from being surrounded by all this potential for pleasure.

She turned away and her gaze scanned the room. Directly to her left were books. Erotic books. The woman from outside was currently browsing the collection, and Bethany yanked her gaze away. This place was intoxicating enough without that distractingly beautiful androgynous women with amazing brown eyes. And anyway, despite how kind she'd been at the very end of their interaction, her earlier crass behaviour meant she was someone Bethany intended to stay well away from, no matter how gorgeous she was.

Beyond the books was a set of shelves holding mugs, coasters, and other sex-themed paraphernalia. A little further clockwise round the room was the dildo section, and directly in front of her, the vibrator section. She knew from researching the shop on the internet that there was also a downstairs area where, if she was so inclined, she could find restraints, whips, paddles, and multiple toys and accessories for anal play.

Maybe another time.

She shivered with excitement. *Definitely* another time, if she ever found the courage to pursue her true desires.

Bethany shuffled forward to the vibrator section, acutely aware that she and the woman she'd spoken to outside were the only customers in the shop. She dared a glance round. The other woman was now in the dildo section, picking up one after the other, hefting them in her hand and turning them every which way before setting them down and moving on to the next. Another sight that threatened to immolate Bethany. She wanted to explore dildos at some point—but again, perhaps not today. And perhaps not until she had a girlfriend to use one on, even though she knew a dildo could just as easily be used for self-pleasuring.

Ripping her gaze away from that section, and specifically the arousing sight of the annoyingly gorgeous woman fondling the silicone dildos, she forced herself to look at the range of vibrators.

The variety was mind-boggling. Thankful again that she'd spent some time in research prior to her visit, her gaze homed in on the two she'd come to see. She picked up one in each hand. They were cool to the touch, but each was intriguing in its own way. Lightweight, and by the looks of it, easy to switch on and off. She turned them over in her hands, part of her brain thrilling at this new level of daring she was displaying. She was in a sex shop, handling vibrators!

"The one on the left is a lovely one."

The voice was close to her ear. Bethany nearly jumped out of her skin, dropped both vibrators, and watched in horror as one thunked at her feet and the other bounced across the wooden floor to land a few feet away.

"God, sorry!" said the voice.

Bethany turned to face the woman.

"You? Again?" Her heart thudding, Bethany swallowed before adding, "You scared the life out of me."

"Um, yeah. Sorry about that."

Bethany sighed and looked to the ceiling, taking a few deep breaths before looking back and saying, "It's okay. Sorry I snapped."

The woman smiled and shrugged. "It's fine. I'm clearly more of a ninja than I realised."

There was a warmth in her manner that had Bethany, in spite of her recent vow, relaxing into their encounter. After all, the woman hadn't done this on purpose. Bethany bent down to pick up the vibrator at her feet, checking it wasn't damaged, and was about to step over to retrieve the other one when the woman touched her arm.

"I'll do that."

She walked over and scooped it up, handing it back to Bethany when she was alongside her again.

"There you go, no damage done."

"Everything okay over there?" the sales assistant called.

"All fine, Mira. Me being a clumsy dolt," the dark-haired woman replied, smiling at Bethany.

"You didn't have to say that," Bethany murmured.

The woman shrugged. "I know."

"Thank you."

She smiled again, and a strange little shiver moved through Bethany's body.

"So, would you like a recommendation, or shall I just back silently away?"

Bethany chuckled, her tension releasing at the self-deprecating joke.

"Um." She paused. *Could she? Should she? Oh, what the hell.* "A recommendation would be helpful, thanks." She blushed. "I-I've never bought one before."

She wasn't entirely sure why she had shared that snippet of information, and especially not with this woman, but it was too late to take it back now.

The woman's eyes widened, and Bethany's blush returned in full force. At twenty-eight, she probably was a little late to the sex-toy party, compared to some. She looked at the woman, trying to assess her age. Probably not far off her own, actually. But clearly more experienced when it came to what was on display in this shop.

"Okay, well in that case, that one would definitely be a great place to start." She pointed at the one in Bethany's left hand. "It's easy to use and has enough levels to satisfy most needs. I bought one myself a few years ago and I still return to it now and again."

Bethany stared. Didn't that count as over-sharing, or were there different rules in a sex shop?

"Sarah's right," Mira said from somewhere behind Bethany. "It's one of our bestsellers for good reason. Lots of women compliment it on its gentle action, especially as a starter vibrator. And it's thin enough that you can use it for vaginal stimulation as well as clitoral."

Bethany swallowed hard and chased away a host of heat-inducing images that flashed through the front of her brain. She looked over her shoulder at Mira, who was smiling warmly.

"Um, okay. Thanks."

She looked back at the woman—*Sarah*—and smiled weakly. "Okay, I think you two have talked me into it."

"Great," Sarah said, smiling yet again. That smile sent a delicious quiver throughout Bethany's body, which annoyed her immensely. *Why am I reacting like this? She was a Neanderthal outside!*

"Cool," Mira said. "I'll get one from the cupboard downstairs and it'll be on the counter when you're ready to pay." She walked past Bethany on her way to the stairs, still smiling.

"Thank you."

Bethany was pleasantly stunned at her own alacrity. Only ten minutes into her first visit to a sex shop and she had her decision made. She placed the two demo vibrators back in their allotted spaces on the shelves, noting the slight trembling of her hands. This was out of her comfort zone, but it didn't mean she didn't want to be here. The realisation had been building over the last few months that something was missing in her life, and that had led her here, as a first step to getting out there again. Wherever 'out there' was. Desire and sexual need had been very much in the back of her mind since college. Since Michelle and their brief time together.

Of course, now that she'd come to accept that she didn't actually want to be alone, and that being involved with someone again would be quite nice, her natural tendency towards geekiness had ensured that she researched the heck out of what that would involve. Knowing her own body, and what she liked or didn't like, was part of it. She had always masturbated—that wasn't the problem. Relying on a few of her favourite fantasies had meant that whenever the urge took her—which wasn't that often—she could happily bring herself to a fairly satisfactory climax. However, some of the research she'd done—films, magazines, books—had opened her eyes, and her libido, to a whole raft of new possibilities.

It felt good, being this adventurous.

"Happy with your purchase?" Sarah asked, and Bethany turned to find her grinning.

Smiling back, the first genuine smile she'd managed since arriving at the shop, Bethany said, "Yes, thank you," and moved away to dare to peruse the rest of the contents on this floor.

"Hey, I never got your name," Sarah called. "Well, I know from outside you're Miss Keane and you teach a little snot called Michael, but I don't know your first name."

Bethany turned back to face her, tilting her head. "Why would you need it?"

Sarah startled, then laughed. "Well, for one thing, you know mine. It only seems fair to know yours."

She edged closer, and her sudden proximity brought her scent to Bethany's nostrils—light, yet musky. Sensuous and teasing. Sparks zapped over Bethany's skin from that scent alone.

"I was also wondering, given how well I talked you into buying a vibrator, if I could also talk you into having a drink with me. There are some great bars around here."

Bethany didn't know whether to be amused or alarmed. At what point in their brief interaction had she given any indication to this woman that she wanted to continue their acquaintance? In fact, surely she'd given every indication she wanted the exact opposite. Bethany knew it had been a while since she'd dipped her toe into the dating pool, but she didn't remember the women she'd known back then being so...forward. And thick-skinned. Or maybe it was just *this* woman.

Bethany took a step back.

"Um, thanks. That's a, um, nice idea, but I'll pass."

There was a slight fall in Sarah's expression, then she seemed to recover and plastered a too-wide smile on her—admittedly, *very* attractive—face. "Okay then. I'll leave you to your shopping." She stepped to the side and theatrically opened her arms to let Bethany pass.

The gesture, in spite of everything, made Bethany smile as she walked past.

"Thank you," she said, dipping her head in a mock bow.

Sarah laughed softly as she walked away.

Wow, I haven't had one blow me off so quickly in ages. But then, I didn't exactly impress her outside the shop, so I suppose I shouldn't be that surprised.

Embarrassment was not an emotion Sarah felt often, but she was knee deep in it now.

Her gaze tracked Miss Keane's movement across the shop to the dildo section. Swearing under her breath, she tamped down any thoughts involving that woman and dildos when they attempted to present themselves to her mind's eye.

Sarah had not actually had a great track record the last few weeks, when she came to think of it. Had she lost her mojo? After working so hard to get herself into such good shape the last few years, she was rather used to women pretty much throwing themselves at her. Such rejection as she'd just experienced was hard to take.

Yeah, and I can just imagine who would say that was good for me.

She snorted, and inhaled a deep breath.

Her gaze, despite her best intentions, insisted on following the delightfully alluring woman who was now lifting dildos of various sizes up from their shelves and turning them in her hands. Sarah tore her gaze away; this level of torture was more than she could bear.

Sarah wasn't even sure what it was about this Miss Keane that had her so hot under the collar. Although, she had to admit, the quiet, geeky type had always been her undoing. It was something about the combination of brains and beauty, and the—often—lack of awareness of exactly how attractive they were.

Or, perhaps, in this case, it was simply the mere fact that the woman seemed immune to her charms.

The thing was, though, she had thought, just for a moment, that Miss Keane's eyes held a slightly different answer. That there was more than a hint of attraction there. She was normally pretty good at reading that stuff, so should she walk away just yet? Would there be any value in having another go?

Sarah sighed. It really wasn't like her to push for a second chance, but, as her gaze drifted once again to where Miss Keane was now handling—actually, more like fondling, *good God*—leather strap-on harnesses, she had to admit the idea was tempting. Sure, the woman hardly seemed the type to meet her deepest needs, but Sarah wasn't sure she was ready to explore that yet anyway. So, just like with all the others, this woman would meet the surface needs, the ones that took only one night to satisfy. If only Sarah could get her to say yes to that drink...

Sarah shook out her shoulders, flexed her fingers, then rolled her neck a couple of times and watched as the woman walked over to the counter to pay for her vibrator. It was her only purchase, Sarah noted, but she was also looking somewhat longingly back over her shoulder at the dildo section.

As she left the counter with her purchase in one of the shop's plain plastic bags, Sarah moved to intercept, keeping her movements smooth and easy. She didn't want to spook her like before.

"Before you go," she said gently, as she reached the woman's shoulder.

Relieved to see Miss Keane stop and turn to look at her, Sarah dipped her hand into the small back pocket of her handbag, where she always kept a stock of her cards. When she withdrew one, the woman looked confused.

"I'm not going to push," Sarah continued, keeping her voice low but friendly, "but I am going to give you my card. I find you very attractive, and I really would like to take you out for that drink one evening. If you change your mind, please call me."

It was bold, but Sarah could do bold. She thrived on it, actually.

Slowly, the woman reached out and took the proffered card, giving Sarah cause for a mental fist pump. She stared at it, then looked back up at Sarah.

"I doubt that's a good idea," she said, her eyes narrowed.

Ouch.

She made to hand the card back, but Sarah, a sense of desperation invading her and making her reckless, reached out and closed the woman's hand over the card, pressing it into her palm.

"Keep it," Sarah said, lowering her voice to her sexiest register. "Just in case you change your mind."

And there it was, that flicker in the woman's eyes again. That hint of something that said she wasn't entirely sure about her denial of Sarah's invitation.

Without a word she shoved the card into her handbag, spun round and walked away, then stopped again as she reached the door. Looking over her shoulder, her hair backlit by the setting sun, she looked...extraordinary. Sarah almost choked in wonder at the vision.

"It's...it's Bethany, by the way," she said, her voice croaky. "My first name." And then she was gone.

CHAPTER 3

SARAH TROTTED UP THE FRONT steps of the imposing Georgian terrace house where her Aunt Evelyn lived and pressed a finger to the old-fashioned bell push. The tinkling of the bell carried out to Sarah's ears, and she smiled. She had fond memories of ringing that bell from her earliest childhood, and spending time with her aunt had been one of the few highlights of Sarah's troubled teenage years.

It wasn't Evelyn who answered, however, but Jonathan, her live-in carer. He'd been with Evelyn for over ten years and was more like a family friend than an employee by this point. At forty-two, he was still handsome and trim, his dark blonde hair kept short to prevent its natural curl from going too wild. He was clean-shaven and lightly tanned, his blue eyes standing out against his tanned skin. He was immaculately dressed as always, in dark jeans and a long-sleeved white T-shirt, although Sarah had to smile at the bright pink household gloves he was wearing.

"Sarah!" He leaned forward to kiss both her cheeks. "She didn't tell me you were coming over."

Sarah returned his embrace before answering. "She doesn't know. I just thought I'd pop round and have a cup of tea."

"Lovely." He stepped aside so she could enter the house. "I'll put the kettle on. She's in the living room."

Sarah thanked him and walked down the airy hallway to the living room. It was her favourite room in the house, furnished in a tasteful style that hinted at money without being crass about it. It had a large window that faced the garden, and the June sunshine was streaming through it.

Her aunt was reading in her favourite chair by the fireplace, although it was too warm a day to need a fire so the grate was empty. Her pale grey hair looked like it had recently been set, and her skin glowed. As usual she wore a smart pair of trousers with a stylish, zipped blue and red cardigan. Evelyn had always had a certain panache about her that made Sarah glow with pride.

"Hi, Evelyn," Sarah called as she walked into the room.

Her aunt raised her head and a wide smile lit up her face.

"Ah, my favourite niece. What a lovely surprise."

She put down her book and stood, using her hands on the arms of the chair to lever herself upright. It took some time, but Sarah didn't offer to help; Evelyn had told her in no uncertain terms on many occasions that she would ask for help if she needed it. Evelyn never asked.

Sarah winced, watching her struggle. It was hard to see her once-active aunt reduced to having difficulty getting out of chairs. She kept forgetting how old Evelyn was now. At eighty-three—ten years older than Sarah's father—her mind was still going strong, but her body was not, much to Evelyn's disgust.

"Come here," Evelyn said, once she was up and steady. She reached out her arms.

Sarah smiled and walked across the room to accept the hug. They held tight to each other for a few moments, then Evelyn pulled away and gestured to the sofa.

"Sit. Tell me all your latest news. Have you had any conquests recently?"

Sarah snorted, and took the proffered seat. "Evelyn, honestly. You can't ask me that."

Evelyn shrugged. "An old lady has to get her kicks somehow, dear."

Sarah shook her head. "You're not old. Well, not much." She grinned as Evelyn gasped in mock horror. "Actually, it's been a quiet few weeks for me on that front."

"Lost your mojo?"

Sarah stared at her. "How do you even know what 'mojo' means?"

"I am a woman of the world, Sarah dear, even if I am stuck in this chair most of the day. I read *The Guardian*. I am familiar with all the latest lingo."

Sarah laughed out loud. "God, Evelyn, you crack me up. Don't ever change."

Evelyn winked. "I do not intend to, dear."

Jonathan appeared, the tray in his hands loaded with all the makings for tea, as well as a plate of biscuits. Placing it on the elegant glass-topped coffee table in front of the sofa, he poured out three cups and passed them round, followed by the plate of biscuits.

"You know I shouldn't," Sarah said, as she pinched two ginger nuts and placed them on the saucer.

Jonathan's gaze performed a once-over sweep of Sarah's body. "Darling, there's not an ounce on you. Trust me, you have room."

He sat next to her. "So, what are we discussing?"

"Sarah's love life," Evelyn replied. "She claims she has nothing to tell us."

Jonathan arched an eyebrow, and Sarah noted with dismay that his were plucked to a perfection she could only dream of.

"Does that mean you may finally have seen the error of your ways? Are you ready to start looking for Ms Right?"

The hopefulness in his voice touched Sarah, but not for long. Long-term relationships were not a possibility for her, not given her history.

"Just having a dry streak," she said but couldn't help wincing when his face dropped. She rushed on, staving off what was certain to be a repeat of his usual lecture. "I did meet a woman last night, though." Sarah directed her comment towards Evelyn, not wishing to see the disappointment in Jonathan's eyes. "She was kind of cute."

Evelyn chortled. "That's my girl. If you fall off the horse, get right back on again."

Jonathan tutted.

"Something to say, Jonathan dear?" Evelyn inquired, her tone snooty.

He turned to Sarah, who steeled herself as she met his gaze. "Another meaningless fling, I presume?"

He almost spat the word 'fling' and Sarah's hackles rose.

"Actually, she turned me down. So there." *Now, why had she admitted that?*

Jonathan smirked. "Hm, maybe you *have* lost your mojo. Or the universe is trying to tell you something."

"Jonathan, I love you like the camp gay brother I never had, but you really need to get off this train."

She picked up one of the ginger nuts and crammed it into her mouth.

"Exactly," Evelyn jumped in, her tone triumphant. "If my darling niece wishes to play the field, she has every right to. Settling down is overrated."

Jonathan put his teacup down on the coffee table and sighed.

"Honestly, Sarah. I despair. You are such a wonderful person. You would make some lucky woman a gorgeous wife." Sarah flinched at the word, but Jonathan ploughed on. "And I don't understand why you keep just sleeping around."

Sarah swallowed her mouthful of biscuit. "Life isn't a Disney movie, Jonathan." Her voice had risen in volume. "Just because you believe in all that Prince Charming crap, and are holding out for a Mr Right to come and sweep you off your feet, doesn't mean that it appeals to the rest of us."

"Hear, hear!" Evelyn chimed.

"And you don't help either," Jonathan said, pointing at Evelyn. "Encouraging her to live this wild life."

Evelyn grinned, her eyes sparkling. "Sarah is a free spirit and she always has been. I merely offer her an alternative viewpoint to your more saccharine take on things."

Jonathan threw his hands up. "Honestly, you two will be the death of me," he said, standing. "What's wrong with romance and love? And happy ever after?"

Sarah reached out and patted his leg. "Nothing," she said, tugging his jeans until he turned round to face her. "For other people. Just not for me."

"But that's the thing that frustrates me the most about all this," he said, pouting. "I actually think it would be exactly what you'd like, if only you'd give it a chance."

Sarah shuddered. "Nope. Definitely not. I'd rather focus on finding you your Prince Charming, actually. There's a gorgeous new guy down in Accounts. I'm convinced he's family. He might be just your type. Well, physically at least."

Jonathan recoiled, his eyes wide. "Oh, no," he said, backing away. "Not another one of your work set ups. I'm not sure I've recovered from the last one."

"Hey look, that wasn't my fault, okay?" Sarah insisted. "How was I supposed to know he was lacking in the personal grooming department?"

"Sarah, he had nose hair longer than his actual nose. How could you not have noticed?"

Evelyn guffawed, and both Sarah and Jonathan turned to look at her.

"Is my torment somehow amusing to you, Evelyn?" Jonathan asked, his tone snide.

"Very," the older woman said, reaching for another biscuit. "This is much better than Saturday night television."

Sarah laughed, and in moments Jonathan was joining in.

"You're a terrible old woman," he said, wagging a finger at Evelyn.

She shrugged. "I know. But I find I do not care."

Jonathan turned to Sarah. "What's a poor gay man to do?"

"She loves you, you know that. She wouldn't have kept you on all these years if she didn't."

There was a harrumph from across the room, and Sarah winked at Jonathan.

He smiled and leaned down to give her a quick hug. "Stay for lunch, as you're here?"

She nodded. "Why not? Thanks."

"Right, I'll go and potter in the kitchen. Throw something together." He paused to look at her, his gaze penetrating, and said quietly, "I meant what I said, you know. I do really think that you'd be happier if you found *the one* and stopped all this shagging around."

Sarah sighed. "I can't, Jonathan. I just…can't."

"What a waste," he said, shaking his head and walking away.

CHAPTER 4

THE COOLED CAKE WAS PRETTY on its stand, the sofa cushions were as plumped as they could be given the age of the things, and the room smelled fresh and sweet from the small vase of freesias on the window sill. Bethany smiled—she was looking forward to her mum's visit. It had been two weeks since they'd seen each other, thanks to conflicts in their schedules, and that was the longest they'd gone all year.

Alice Keane was possibly Bethany's favourite person in the world. Her mother was intelligent, witty, and had cheerfully raised her brood of three almost single-handedly since her husband died when Bethany was nine. Alice had never remarried, never even looked. Robert Keane had been her *one*, she said, and you only got one of those in a lifetime. Alice had had plenty of help in those first few years after his death in bringing up their children—both she and Robert came from large families, so Bethany and her siblings had a mass of aunties, uncles and cousins. Bethany had been surrounded by family for as long as she could remember, but it was always her mother who held the biggest place in her heart.

When the buzzer rang she pressed the intercom button to let her in, and opened the front door to her flat just as her mum was climbing the stairs up from the ground floor hallway. She was looking good in cropped jeans and thin sweater, her thick brown hair pinned back with a barrette.

"Hello, love," Alice said, her smile wide.

"Hi, Mum. So glad you're here."

They hugged on the doorstep, then Bethany led the way into the living room. Her mum sat on the sofa, while Bethany popped the kettle on in the adjoining kitchen and came back to talk while it boiled.

"How have you been?"

"Not too bad, love. Working my behind off, of course."

"Of course." Bethany smiled and shook her head. Her mum had a part-time job and served in a voluntary basis on the board of a local community group, and although she complained constantly about being overworked, Bethany knew she wouldn't have it any other way. Alice revelled in being useful.

"And you? Work still okay? The little buggers haven't defeated you yet?"

Bethany chuckled. "No, and they never will. I love them."

"You're a saint," her mum muttered. "I couldn't do it."

"Actually, I think you could. You did a great job with me and my brothers, after all."

"That's different—you were my own, so I could shout at you as much as I liked when you did something insane or dangerous. Doubt it would be the same with other people's children."

"Yes, you do have a point there." Bethany laughed. "I'm very good at counting to ten under my breath." She stood as she heard the kettle reach its zenith in the kitchen. "Back in a tick."

She made a large pot of tea—she and her mother were always two cups kind of women when they got together—and brought it out on a tray with a proper little milk jug and sugar bowl. Then she turned back to the kitchen to retrieve the cake, and was rewarded with a pleasing "oooh" when she placed it on the small table in front of the sofa.

"That looks delicious," her mum said, rubbing her hands together.

"I hope so." Bethany handed her the knife. "Care to do the honours?"

"Always."

Alice cut into the red velvet cake, carving out a generous slice for each of them and transferring the pieces with care to the small plates Bethany had brought out on the tea tray.

They munched on the cake and sipped their tea for a couple of minutes, content in their comfortable silence.

"So, what else is going on in your world?" Alice asked.

"Oh, not much."

Except for going to a sex shop, buying a vibrator, and being propositioned by a gorgeous but completely irritating woman who acted like I was some pathetic damsel in need of saving.

"What?" Her mum was staring intently. "There's something you're not telling me."

Damn it. Alice had always been far too good at that. She could always lie, of course. But this was her mother.

"Um, so I kind of got asked out last night."

Yes, let's focus on that bit rather than the rest of it.

Alice smiled wide and slapped her free hand down on her knee. "That's fantastic! When are you seeing her?"

"Whoa, Mum, let's slow down a little. I didn't actually say yes."

"What?" Her mum's face fell comically, from joy to dismay in less than a second. "Was she ugly?"

Bethany had just taken the last small bite of her piece of cake and nearly snorted it out through her nose.

"Mum!" She shook her head. "No, she wasn't ugly. Far from it, actually."

"Okay, young lady, start at the beginning."

Bethany sighed. It was worse than the Spanish Inquisition when her mum got started like this, and she knew there'd be no escape from telling her the whole truth. Her cheeks warmed in anticipation. Maybe she could keep the fact that a sex shop was involved out of the discussion…

"Okay, so I went shopping on the way home from work. I first met her outside, and she was just, God, so cocky and full of herself and, ugh, really irritating. Then I dropped my handbag and suddenly she was really helpful and…nice. Then I was in the shop, comparing two….products to see which one I preferred and she, Sarah, offered me some advice."

"Advice? Who gives advice in a shop to a virtual stranger?"

Oh, God. Her mum was like a terrier with a bone when a story didn't quite add up.

"Um, well, it was kind of a specialist shop, and she had, you know, specialist knowledge."

"Right." Her mum drew the word out, looking sceptical.

Oh, bloody hell.

"Look, it was…it was a sex shop, Mum."

Bethany's cheeks were on fire, and the heat spread to her neck within moments.

Alice blinked twice, and her mouth made a strange little contorted shape before she took a deep breath and said, "Go on."

Pressing her palms to her face to try to lower the heat it was emitting, which could have boiled them another pot of tea if it continued, Bethany breathed in before carrying on with the story.

"It's a great shop, not one of those seedy places in Soho," she said quickly, noticing her mum's raised eyebrows. "It's women-run, and it's very welcoming to lesbians."

Alice nodded, sipping her tea.

"So, well, I was looking at something—please don't make me tell you what it was—and Sarah offered me her advice and then, well, she said she found me very attractive and she'd like to ask me out for a drink."

"And you said no?" There was no judgement in her mum's tone, merely curiosity.

Bethany exhaled. "It really threw me. I mean, for starters, she was beyond annoying at first. Plus we'd only just met. I know nothing about her, except she's gorgeous, and clearly knows her way around a sex shop."

Alice snorted, and clapped a hand over her mouth.

Bethany scowled at her.

"And, you know, I'm only just getting used to the idea of dating again, so I'm not going to accept just the first offer that comes my way, am I? Especially when I got such confusing signals from her."

"Well." Alice shrugged. "I mean, unless you got any kind of vibe off Sarah that she was a bit, you know, weird, why not go for that drink with her?"

"Really? Even after she irritated me?"

Alice laughed. "It sounds to me like she redeemed herself with her, um, advice."

Bethany blushed again, her mind suddenly filled with images of Sarah—her strong, beautiful face, her gorgeous smile.

"What?" Alice asked, bringing Bethany back to the present.

"What?"

"You disappeared on me for a moment there."

"Oh. Well. Yes." She cleared her throat. "I was just kind of thinking about her."

Alice smiled. "That's a shame given that you turned her down. Well, I'm sure there will—"

"She gave me her card."

Alice's smile froze on her face. "Oh, she did, did she?"

Bethany nodded, her mind working a mile a minute.

"So, are you going to call her?" Alice's tone was overly casual as she reached for the last bite of her cake and mopped up the crumbs with a wet fingertip. "Mm, so good," she mumbled.

"Thank you. I always enjoy making a red velvet."

"And avoiding my questions," Alice said with a smirk.

"I wasn't avoiding, Mum. Merely…stalling," she admitted, and laughed when Alice threw her a death stare, her hazel eyes narrowed. "Okay. So, yes, I am considering calling her."

"Okay." Alice reached for the teapot and refilled both their cups. "Why not? You don't have to look at it as a date. You can just take it as it is, one drink with someone you got talking to in a shop. I mean, the fact that it was a sex shop doesn't have to mean anything."

She smirked and Bethany blushed.

"And here I am regretting that I tell you everything," Bethany said, shaking her head.

Alice smiled and patted her hand indulgently. "We're both adults, love." Her face turned serious. "And I hope you know you *can* tell me anything. Any time you need someone to listen. You know I would never judge."

Bethany nodded, squeezing her mother's hand. "I know. Thank you."

And it was true. Her mum had always been her best support, and Bethany had never felt embarrassed about sharing with her. Alice had even been the one to suggest to Bethany, when she was fourteen, that her sexual orientation may not be entirely straight, therefore removing any drama Bethany may have had around coming out as lesbian when she finally decided that was her label at nineteen.

"So, any chance of another slice of that?" Alice asked, pointing at the cake even as she reached for the knife.

Bethany laughed, and pushed her own plate towards her mum. "Only if you cut one for me too."

Bethany ran the rolling pin lightly over the scone mixture until it had been massaged into a flat pancake of dough just under an inch deep. Setting the rolling pin aside, she picked up the crimped cutter and pressed it into the dough, popping out the two-inch round and placing it onto the prepared baking sheet. She hummed as she worked, and pushed her glasses up with the back of her hand when they threatened to slip down her nose.

Baking was her go-to stress reliever. Not that she was stressed, per se, not really. Edgy was more like it.

Nervous.

After her visit with her mum the day before, she had stared at Sarah's card umpteen times where it sat on her tiny coffee table, taunting her.

This morning, after a rather fitful sleep, she had set to work on baking a marmalade cake and now this batch of scones, both for the staffroom at the primary school where she worked. Her fellow teachers were always grateful for their Monday morning treats, and Bethany's mood calmed in anticipation of seeing their smiling faces in a little under twenty-four hours. She loved her job, and part of that revolved around her wonderful co-workers. She knew she was lucky; some of the teacher training peers she kept in touch with had regaled her with horror stories of not-so-nice colleagues in other schools.

She pushed the full baking sheet into the oven, started the timer, and then washed her hands before slipping out of her apron and reaching for her mug of coffee. The sofa accepted her with a small groan, the cushions giving more than they should and requiring her to shift a few times until her backside found a spot that didn't involve a spring poking uncomfortably into soft flesh.

Next purchase. Two more months and I should have enough saved.

The coffee was the perfect temperature and she savoured the intense flavour. Her gaze drifted once again to Sarah's card:

Sarah Connolly, Senior Legal Advisor, Robbins & Pearse Ltd

So, she was a lawyer. Which meant she was smart. Bethany hadn't Googled the company just yet, but the card was good quality, embossed, and therefore not cheap. Sarah probably earned much more than she did. Would that be a problem? Bethany was fiercely independent, and would always wish to pay her own way in any transaction, be that with a friend, family member or...partner.

She shook her head at herself—she was getting carried away. They hadn't even had that first drink yet.

Her mum was right; unless she talked to Sarah, she'd never know if a better personality went with those amazing looks. Or if Sarah's intelligence was as high as her job would suggest. Or if money would or wouldn't be an issue between them.

And if one drink went well, maybe they could try dinner next. Bethany's mind drifted again. And if that went well, perhaps a picnic, or a visit to a museum. Would Sarah even like museums? Or picnics?

She put down her mug and stood up. There was only one way to find out.

A trickle of sweat rolled down the back of Sarah's neck, and she grinned, standing up on her pedals to give the simulated hill climb the energy it deserved. She was panting, and her quads were screaming, but the endorphins flooding her system meant pure joy ran through her body rather than pain.

She'd drifted off with her thoughts while riding, her mind, much to her surprise, returning to her interlude with Bethany at the shop on Friday night rather than her pleasant afternoon with Evelyn and Jonathan, only yesterday. Something about Bethany kept tugging at her. It was inexplicable—after getting shot down by a woman, something that rarely happened anyway, Sarah usually forgot about them and moved on. But not so with Bethany, and this puzzled her. Maybe she should hit one of the clubs next weekend, see about breaking this poor run she was on.

The timer on the exercise bike reached her thirty-minute target and the bike slowed into cool down mode. She flopped back onto the saddle and eased the pace of her legs, her arms folded on the frame in front of her. If someone had told her in her early teens—when she had hated PE lessons with a passion and did all she could not to take part in any sports events at school—that she'd be sitting here now relishing the afterglow of her workout, she would have laughed in their faces.

Her phone rang and she snatched it up from its perch on the little shelf built into the bike's handle bars. Caller display showed her aunt's name.

"Hi, Evelyn, everything okay?"

"Hello, Sarah. You sound out of breath—am I interrupting anything?"

There was a smirk in her aunt's voice and Sarah grinned.

"No, you dirty old woman. I've just finished a workout on the bike."

"Good. I am pleased that it is still making such a difference to you."

"Yep, it is. You can totally take the credit for that."

"Yes, well, it was that or pay for your rehab, dear. The bicycle was cheaper."

Sarah laughed out loud, but her stomach flipped at the truth of Evelyn's words. Evelyn had without doubt rescued Sarah from a deep, dark pit of over-indulgence and life-wasting behaviour some years ago, and Sarah would always be grateful for that.

"True. Anyway," she rushed on, before emotion overwhelmed her, "what can I do for you? I only saw you yesterday."

"I know, but I blame my age. I forgot to remind you about the charity dinner this week. You are still coming with me, yes?"

"Of course! Wouldn't miss it for anything."

Evelyn, like many women with substantial means, supported a variety of charities and actually had a seat on the board of a few. Sarah was often her partner for their swanky events, where she enjoyed seeing Evelyn back in her element, the centre of attention, entertaining everyone within earshot. While they tended to tire Evelyn out now, she still sparkled during these events, and it brought deep joy to Sarah to see her aunt so lit up.

"Excellent. I shall see you on Wednesday then. Seven o'clock sharp."

"Yes, ma'am!"

Evelyn chuckled and hung up.

Sarah reached for the small towel tucked into the waistband at the back of her shorts and wiped down her sweaty face before climbing down off the bike and heading towards the bathroom.

Her apartment boasted the kind of bathroom normally reserved for classy hotels, and it was one of the main reasons she'd purchased the flat some four years ago. The mortgage had stretched her back then, but two promotions in three years had eased that financial burden somewhat. As she crossed the apartment, bright morning sunshine spilled into the open-plan lounge, kitchen, and dining area from the double doors that led out to the balcony. And that was the other main reason she'd bought the flat—the view from that small outside space, overlooking the water, was sublime.

As she reached the bathroom, her phone trilled from where she'd only just left it on the kitchen counter. She could have let it go to voicemail but something pulled her across the room to at least see who was calling, thinking that perhaps it was Evelyn again with another forgotten reminder.

It was, however, an unrecognised number. Normally she would let such a call go to voicemail for sure, but inexplicably her hand was reaching out to swipe the 'Answer' button and her mouth was saying, "Hello?"

"Um, hi. Sarah?"

The voice sounded vaguely familiar, but she couldn't place it. "Yes. Who is this?"

"Hi. It's…it's Bethany. From the s-shop on Friday evening."

The fading glow from her exercise returned in full force.

Well, well, well.

"Hello, Bethany-from-the-shop. How lovely to hear from you."

Bethany gave a half-laugh. "Yes. Well. I was, er, thinking about what you said. About going for a drink. I was wondering if you were still interested."

Her voice held more than a hint of nerves, and Sarah found herself wanting to tread far more lightly than she would have done with anyone else.

"Of course," she said, softening her tone, taking the teasing lilt out of it. "I definitely am. I'm very happy you called."

"Oh. Good."

There was a long silence, and Sarah wondered if Bethany had used up all her confidence in simply making this call in the first place. In which case, Sarah had confidence in abundance and was happy to give things a shove.

"It might be short notice, but are you free this evening by any chance?"

There was a sound like a little squeak.

"Um, yes, actually. That would be f-fine."

"Great." Sarah pondered the little jig of joy her stomach performed, then pushed it aside. "So, whereabouts are you based? I'm in Limehouse."

"Oh, I'm in Finchley, but I'm close to the Tube so I can meet you anywhere, really."

"Well, why don't we choose somewhere roughly in the middle between us, so neither of us has to travel too far?"

"Sounds good. But, um, you'll need to suggest somewhere as I don't really know where to go."

How cute. Once again something wriggled in Sarah's belly, something pleasant and warm and…satisfying, in a way she couldn't describe.

She had to swallow before speaking. "Right, well, there's a nice wine bar I know just off Long Acre in Covent Garden. We could meet at around seven. Does that sound okay?"

What was happening to her? Normally she wasn't so…solicitous. Normally she would just say when and where they were meeting and expect the woman to concur. She never checked to see if they were happy with the suggestion.

"That sounds fine. Could you text me the address?"

"Of course."

"Okay. Great. That's…great."

"Bethany," Sarah said softly, enjoying how the forming of the name felt on her tongue.

"Yes?"

"Thank you very much for calling."

"Oh. Oh, okay. See you tonight."

Something in Bethany's tone told Sarah she was blushing, and that gave Sarah a buzz of something thrilling she couldn't begin to understand.

As Sarah put down her phone, she was aware she was smiling. But it wasn't her usual lascivious smile, of hunger and anticipation. Instead, it was happy; content.

It felt both wonderful and strange, all at the same time.

CHAPTER 5

BETHANY WAS—GENERALLY—A CALM, LEVEL-HEADED WOMAN who knew what she wanted and worked hard to get it. She had been utterly focused in school and college, thrilling in her own intelligence and the opportunities it presented to her. Her teachers had all praised her drive and hard work. And while they'd pointed out that she was shy and could do with speaking up more in class, no one pushed too hard. Bethany was quiet at home too—having two loud and energetic brothers ensured that her voice was rarely heard above their ruckus. She held her own though, when needs be, and her mother had always encouraged her to do so whenever appropriate.

Her current state, therefore, was annoying, to say the least. She had stumbled her way through that call, blushing and stuttering until she wanted to groan in frustration at how inept and immature she must have seemed to the perfectly poised and confident Sarah. Yes, it had been years since she'd been on a date, and yes, of course it was natural to be a tad nervous about it. But turning into a shaking mess was not the way to approach it.

Woman up! Sarah is just another human being whom you will share one drink with to see if you are in any way compatible for exploring further possibilities. She is not some goddess who needs to be venerated and genuflected to.

The pep talk helped; her breathing became less ragged and her heart rate slowed. The words, however, did nothing to sort out the pile of discarded outfits and matching accessory options on the bed in front of her.

Just pick something. Anything.

She reached forward. The yellow sundress with the blue flowers on it would do. And maybe the bold colour would engender confidence that she, Bethany Keane, could in fact go on her first date in nearly eight years.

Dressing quickly, she observed her reflection in the full-length mirror on the inside door of her wardrobe. *Okay, not too bad.* She lifted her shoulders, feeling taller. The hint of cleavage at the neckline was sexy without being too revealing—she hoped—and her bare legs didn't look too pale against the brightness of the dress, even with the dark blue sandals that adorned her feet. She pulled a short navy blue cardigan out of the pile of clothes and slipped it on. With a small clutch in her hand, she was ready, at last.

She sucked in a deep breath and left the house.

When she exited the Tube at Leicester Square, the butterflies started to take flight in her stomach. Unfortunately, it didn't take more than five minutes to find the wine bar, which gave her nerves no time to calm. Seeing Sarah sitting at a small table near the window only heightened them. She looked amazing—her scarlet top hung a little off her shoulders and dipped teasingly low across her chest. She wore what looked like diamond studs in her ears, which twinkled as they caught the evening light through the window of the bar, and a chunky silver ring on her left hand. Her hair was styled slightly differently, the front swept more to one side than before, and it made her look even more glamorous than Bethany remembered.

She swallowed as Sarah saw her and waved. Okay, it appeared she was really doing this.

The bar wasn't noisy when she walked in; soft jazz played over the sound system, but it wasn't intrusive. Sarah stood as Bethany approached, and the gesture touched her.

"Bethany," Sarah breathed her name as if it was an incantation, and it sent shivers spiralling down Bethany's spine. "You look amazing." Sarah's eyes were shining, her smile wide.

"Thank you." Bethany sat in the chair opposite, placing her clutch on the table. "So do you," she said, daring to take a lingering look at Sarah, who smiled in return.

There was a drinks menu on the table.

"Have you chosen already?" Bethany asked, gesturing to it.

"I have, but I haven't ordered yet. I wanted to wait for you." Sarah's brow creased into a small frown at her own words, as if, somehow, they'd not been quite what she expected to say.

"Well, that's very thoughtful of you. Thank you."

Bethany lifted the menu and quickly perused the white wines sold by the glass. Upon choosing a Pinot Grigio, she looked up to find Sarah staring at her, a faint smile on her lips. Bethany flushed under the attention even as it made her glow inside.

The waitress appeared, absolving Bethany from any sort of response. Sarah opted for a Malbec, and the choice of something so strong and robust did not surprise Bethany. It was a wine that suited what she already knew of Sarah.

They swapped small talk until their wine was delivered. Touching glasses, they each took a sip, emitting small moans of appreciation as they savoured their chosen libations, and laughing after they did so.

"Are you a wine connoisseur?" Sarah asked, smiling.

"Not particularly. I know what I like and what I don't like. I've always wanted to take a trip to Italy, or maybe Spain, solely to tour the vineyards."

"Mm, that sounds like a wonderful idea. I went to South Africa a couple of years ago, and did some winery tours there. It was fun, but also very interesting. They really try to teach you rather than let you just quaff down all day."

"Whereabouts in South Africa?"

Bethany listened, entranced, as Sarah spoke enthusiastically about her travels. They swapped stories of places they had been or would like to go. For Bethany, the latter list was considerably longer than the former, and she cringed slightly when Sarah picked up on that fact.

"So, it sounds like you haven't been able to travel as much as you'd like. Is that because of work?"

Bethany nodded slowly, wondering just how honest to be.

As honest as possible, as early as possible, if you want to start things off on the right foot.

"Um, yes. I'm a teacher, as you may have gathered, so not only do I have to fit my holidays around school terms, but because of that it means I can only go at peak times, and a teacher's salary doesn't often stretch that far."

"What do you teach?"

Bethany smiled in gratitude; Sarah hadn't offered sympathy or pity, neither of which she could have stomached.

"I'm a primary school teacher, so a lot of everything for kids that age."

"Oh, that's the cutest age, right? Before they turn into little bast—demons. Although," she said, tilting her head, "you already have at least one little bast—demon in your class, yes?"

Bethany snorted at the correction. "You can swear, it's okay."

Sarah smiled and wiped her brow in an exaggerated *phew* motion.

"Yes, little Michael is…challenging, to say the least. They're not all exactly angels at this age, believe me," Bethany said with a chuckle. "But mostly, yes, they are very sweet and can say the most adorable things."

And she was off, chatting about her work, answering Sarah's intelligent questions. Before she knew it, she'd reached the end of her glass of wine.

Sarah pointed at her own empty glass. "Shall we get another?"

"Yes, please," Bethany replied without hesitation, and Sarah beamed.

"Wait, you named your car Frannie?" Sarah laughed and leaned forward in her chair. "Seriously?"

Bethany smirked, and it gave Sarah a warm glow inside. Bethany was opening up, relaxing, and it was wonderful to observe. She reminded Sarah of a shy creature emerging from its shell, and Sarah was pleased she'd helped that process start.

"She's a Ford Fiesta, and Frannie just kind of…fits." Bethany sighed. "She's getting old now, though. And I can't really afford to replace her so when she goes, I'll probably give up a car altogether."

"I don't have one. I've never bothered, living in London."

"Yes, I know lots of Londoners don't. I just got used to having her when I was at university; plus, she was a present from my mum, so I just couldn't give her up once I moved back to take up my teaching job."

Sarah couldn't really understand but she nodded anyway. Attachment to 'things' had not played a major part in her life. Sure, she'd never wanted for anything, with her parents as well off as they were, but maybe that was it—everything had been too easy to obtain, and so its emotional or sentimental value was minimal. Presumably Bethany's mum giving her a car was a big deal in their relationship, so of course it meant more.

"...and going away to study was a big thing."

Shit. She'd tuned out, and now sat upright to bring herself back into the conversation. How much had she missed? And just what the hell was happening to her tonight? She never lost attention on a date. Never.

Quick, think of a question!

"Did you settle into uni life okay though?"

Bethany shrugged. "I did, after a few months. Luckily Bristol was a big enough town that there were plenty of things to do once I did find my feet."

Good. Saved.

Bethany started talking about her classes, and her fellow students, using her hands to emphasise certain points, her recollections of her time at uni clearly bringing her joy. Sarah leaned her elbow on the table and propped her chin in her hand, mesmerised by the beautiful sight in front of her.

The wine was making her mellow, yes, but she knew most of this wonderful state of being came from sharing time with Bethany. From talking to her, laughing with her, merely being in her presence. A number of times Sarah had tried to shake it off, to get back into her tried and trusted game zone, but even trying to remember what that was eluded her.

Was Bethany some kind of witch? Had she cast a spell over Sarah? It was weird, like everything Sarah normally did and said during a date in order to lead the evening to its ultimate—and usually very pleasurable—conclusion had been removed from her brain. She tried pinching herself, to pull herself out of this haze where everything was warm, and cosy, and dreamy.

Then, out of the corner of her eye, she saw someone whose mere presence instantly pulled her into a full state of alertness. *Oh, shit. Kristen.* Sarah tried turning slightly, so the back of her head would be presented to the rest of the bar, but it was too late. Kristen slid off her stool and began to make her way over.

"Are you okay?" Bethany asked, tilting her head slightly.

"Ah, no, not really. I apologise in advance for—"

"Sarah." The word dripped with ice. "Fancy seeing you here."

Sarah winced and turned to face the visitor, trying at the same time to ignore the evident shock on Bethany's face.

"Kristen. You're looking well. But if you'll excuse me, I'm actually here with—"

Kristen turned to look at Bethany and Sarah's stomach plummeted. "Yes, so I see. I assume this is your latest conquest? Look out, whoever you are. Don't expect coffee in the morning. You'll be lucky if she's still in the bed when you wake up."

Sarah's heart thudded. "Kristen! Please, there's no need for that."

"Really?" Kristen's eyebrows arched. She was still beautiful—that tall, lithe body perfect in its proportions, her blonde hair ridiculously long and soft-looking, but the blue eyes were harder than Sarah remembered, and the mouth that had been so plump to kiss now looked thin and cruel.

Sarah stood. Enough was enough. "Kristen," she hissed, staring intently into her eyes, "leave it. I never made you any promises, and you know that. Please, walk away and leave me and my date alone."

Kristen visibly flinched at the word 'date,' and snorted softly. "Whatever. Good luck," she spat at Bethany, then stalked away.

Sarah closed her eyes for a moment before turning back to the table and sliding into her chair. Bethany's face was a mix of confusion and anger.

"Bethany," Sarah said, keeping her tone as even as she could manage given how much her insides were churning. "I am so sorry about that."

"Who was she?" Bethany's tone was hard, and Sarah couldn't blame her.

Sighing, Sarah took a fortifying sip of her wine before speaking. "A woman I had a one-night stand with about three months ago." She had no desire to lie to Bethany, and she had no idea why that was so. "It seems she misunderstood my intentions that night and was very angry about me leaving in the morning. Normally I handle things like that better but somehow I got that one wrong."

Bethany sat as far back in her chair as possible, her left hand fiddling with her handbag where it lay on the table. She looked ready to bolt.

"Normally? Is that what I am? A one-night stand?"

Sarah stared at her. How the hell did she answer that? *As honestly as you answered her first question*, a little voice somewhere in the back of her head said.

"When I asked you for your number on Friday, yes, that was my intention. It isn't now."

She flushed, and her stomach dropped to her knees and back again. Cold sweat broke out across her shoulder blades. She'd meant it. Every word. *Holy shit.*

Bethany blinked, and took a sip of her wine. Then she grimaced. "Well, I can't fault you for honesty." She turned to look out the window.

Sarah waited.

When Bethany looked back, there was a firm resolution in her eyes. "Okay. I'll stay. But let's see how we are at the end of the evening before we think beyond tonight."

Sarah's relief was a hot and cold wave of feeling flowing through her veins. "Thank you. And again, I'm very sorry for how that unfolded."

Bethany shrugged. "You couldn't have anticipated it."

They were silent for a moment.

"At the risk of sounding like I'm just trying to feed you a line right now," Sarah said, her voice sounding nervy even to her own ears, "I was really having a great time with you before that, and it's been lovely getting to know a little bit about you."

Bethany smiled—it was small, but it was a start. "Me too." She sighed and leaned forward. "Okay, let's forget that woman, shall we? We're here, we've got wine, let's not waste it."

Sarah chuckled, shaking her head. "You are one cool customer, Bethany Keane."

Bethany's answering laughter was musical. "Okay, flattery may yet work."

Sarah rubbed her hands together. "Great. Let me work on that. In the meantime, I believe you were telling me about your uni days. You were the serious one, yes?"

Seemingly willing to take up Sarah's unspoken offer to reset the evening right back to where it had been so rudely side-tracked, Bethany grinned.

"Yes, I'm afraid I was one of those very studious types in college; no partying."

"Always the one with her nose in her books and her homework in on time?"

"Exactly!" Bethany blushed, her cheeks turning the sweetest of pinks.

"No naughty Sapphic escapades in the halls after dark?"

Bethany frowned. "Well, even if I did, I'm not sure I'd share that sort of tale with you on our first date."

Sarah winced. The flirty question had just slipped out, as per usual, and Bethany's reaction made it abundantly clear that that wasn't her style. *Don't be an asshole. There's something different about her compared to all the women who have gone before, so* you *have to be different too.* Sarah feared she wasn't up to the task.

"Sorry about that. I…" She sighed and plunged on, hoping Bethany would re-engage with a serious question. "Are you still studying, perhaps for a Masters?"

Bethany's shoulders relaxed, and Sarah inwardly breathed a sigh of relief. "No, all done. I qualified and have been teaching for five years now."

"Good for you!" Sarah toasted her with the last of her wine.

Bethany smiled, then said, "Um, I was wondering, do they do food here? This wine is going to my head and I think I need to eat something."

"We could always go back to my place. I'm sure we could find something to eat there. Each other, perhaps." She smirked, and in the next moment knew the comment had dropped her straight back into the asshole zone.

Bethany froze, her eyes narrowing and her lips pursing. "You can't seem to help yourself, can you?" she said, her tone clipped. "I thought you'd redeemed your Neanderthal persona when you were so nice inside the shop, but now I'm thinking that was all a bit of an act."

"Neanderthal?" Sarah's hackles rose, although she knew it was more from anger at herself than at Bethany.

"Yes!" Bethany snapped, before she reached into her handbag and yanked out some money, which she then threw on the table. "Crass jokes and comments, acting all macho. It might work on women like Kristen but not on me." Her voice was a hiss from between tight lips, and her eyes blazed. She looked incredible all riled up, but Sarah set that observation aside as she scrambled to rescue the situation.

"Bethany, I'm sorry. I—"

Bethany stood, and Sarah rose to block her exit.

"Bethany, please. I really am sorry." Bethany wouldn't meet her gaze. "Look, yes, I agree, some of my comments have been misguided. I…" She groaned, knowing how bad this was going to sound but knowing she had to say it. "It's what I've always done, and it's always got me what I wanted in the past. I'm not going to hide from that. But there really is something about you that makes me want to be different. I—"

"Sarah, please let me pass." Bethany's tone was unforgiving, and she still wouldn't meet Sarah's eyes.

Sarah sighed. "Bethany, please. Give me another chance."

Well, this was certainly new territory, begging a woman to stay. But she had to; there was something about this woman, something that had Sarah convinced she would lose something very important if Bethany left right now.

Bethany said nothing, but she did, at last, raise her head to lock eyes with Sarah. There was hurt in her expression, and confusion, and sorrow, and all of it turned the wine sour in Sarah's stomach.

"I really do want to be different with you," Sarah whispered, then sighed as Bethany pushed past her and walked out of the bar.

CHAPTER 6

SLAM! THE FILING CABINET DRAWER rammed into place with a satisfyingly loud metallic clang.

"Hey, Connolly, what's with the attitude?"

It was Roy, the other senior legal advisor at Robbins & Pearse Ltd—Sarah's only peer, and a man she detested with every fibre of her being.

"Time of the month?" he asked, a sneer in his tone.

"Piss off," Sarah muttered under her breath before turning to face him. "Don't know what you mean," she said blithely, before walking back to her cubicle across from his, the folder she'd retrieved from the cabinet gripped tightly in her hand, bearing the brunt of her anger.

Roy grunted and swivelled in his chair back to his monitor. Sarah had learned long ago the secret to taking the wind out of his sails whenever he felt the need to confront her: ignore him, not rise to the bait, and walk away.

She threw the folder down on her desk and flopped into her chair, swivelling it slowly left and right as her gaze drifted out of the tenth-floor window that overlooked Liverpool Street station. She watched without really seeing as the people below scurried in and out, their lives ticking along, presumably just as they always did.

Hers wasn't, and that was what had her in such a foul mood this morning.

The date with Bethany had been wonderful. Amazing. Unforgettable.

Right up to the point where Sarah had reverted to her flirty—some might say obnoxious—self and completely blown it.

She was mad at herself, but also a little mad at Bethany for not giving her another chance. Sure, Sarah *had* been a little crass in her comments, but most women would have rolled their eyes at her, or given some witty comeback and just moved on with the evening. Sarah's apology had been sincere, but had fallen on deaf ears, and she couldn't help feeling that Bethany had walked away too easily.

Vaguely aware that Roy was now walking away towards the coffee station, Sarah dropped her head back, huffing out a breath as she stared at the ceiling. She needed to talk to someone. It was hard to accept, but she was way out of her depth with this thing.

Her mobile was buried deep in her handbag, but eventually her fingers closed around it and she pulled it out.

Evelyn answered after only two rings.

"Sarah, dear. What a lovely surprise in the middle of a day."

"Hi, Evelyn. How are you?"

"I'm very well. Just completed today's crossword and Jonathan's now making us some lunch before we tackle that pesky viburnum."

Sarah smiled—Evelyn's true passion in life was her garden. It was small but beautiful, packed full of plants, and although her body was slowing down, her enthusiasm wasn't. If there was a task she couldn't manage herself, Jonathan—or sometimes Sarah—was roped in to carry out her commands, which she issued from a comfortable chair on the small paved area just outside the kitchen door.

"Well I'm glad to hear you're keeping him busy."

Evelyn chuckled.

"Anyway," Sarah continued, her voice cracking slightly. "I was wondering if you were around tonight."

"I am, yes. Would you like to come for dinner?"

"If that's not imposing or too last minute?"

"Not at all, dear. I will tell Jonathan."

"Thanks, Evelyn."

"Everything okay, Sarah?" Evelyn's voice held concern.

Sarah sighed. "I don't know. I need to talk to you about something. About a woman."

"Oh, well in that case, get here as soon as you can, dear. Can you get away for lunch?"

The unmistakeable sounds of Roy's annoying whistling drifted down the corridor and Sarah knew he was on his way back to his desk.

"Sorry, I can't do lunch. I'll see you this evening, okay? Gotta go."

"All right, dear. See you later." Evelyn's disappointment was obvious, but Sarah couldn't help that. She did allow herself a wry chuckle, though—reaching out for advice to her ageing aunt and her waspish carer might not be the best idea she'd had all week, but whatever they came up with, it was sure to be entertaining.

Roy returned with the gorgeous guy from Accounts trailing after him.

"Visitor for you," Roy grunted, thumbing in the guy's direction. "Didn't know where your cubicle was," he finished, his tone dripping with sarcasm. He rolled his eyes before walking off again.

"Tosser," Sarah muttered, then looked at the man standing before her. Much to his credit, he wore a friendly grin, despite Roy's less than stellar introduction. He was about her height, with light brown hair combed into a neat wave, and was smartly dressed in a dark blue suit. His chiselled chin was the sort she'd only ever seen in old Hollywood movies, and he was rather breath-taking when he smiled.

Holding out his hand, he said, "Hi, Scott Fisher. I work on the forecasting and budgeting team."

Sarah shook his hand and returned the smile. "Nice to meet you. And sorry about…" She gestured vaguely in the direction Roy had taken.

Scott chuckled. "Don't worry, I've worked with worse than him."

I find that hard to believe.

"So, what can I do for you, Scott?"

"I just wanted to check a couple of contracts with you; make sure I understand the penalty clauses. We've got some issues with a supplier and we're currently holding off paying their last three invoices. I need to know if I have to factor a hefty fine into our next forecasting cycle if we refuse to pay."

"Cool. Take a seat and we'll go through them."

Scott was a breath of fresh air in her otherwise stale morning. He was intelligent, easily following her explanations of the trickier penalty clauses, and although obviously not her type—being a man and all—he certainly was far nicer to look at than most. His eyes, in particular, were a beautiful hazel that seemed to glow in the bright sunshine that streamed through the window.

When they were done, Scott thanked her profusely.

"And remember, don't let the dinosaur get you down," he said conspiratorially as he stood, and his mouth creased into a gentle smirk.

She smiled, but it fell away as he departed. Dinosaur. Didn't Bethany think Sarah belonged in prehistory? *Ugh, don't tell me I have something in common with Roy.*

"Michael! Put that stick down. Right now!" Bethany rolled her eyes as he defiantly hurled the stick into the hedge that lined the back of the playground. "Little bastard," she muttered.

A chuckle from her right told her she'd been heard. Luckily it was only Elise, her colleague on playground duty this lunchtime.

"That he is," Elise concurred. She closed the distance between them, and nudged Bethany with her shoulder. "Hey, are you okay today? You seem a little…rattled."

Bethany sighed. "Sorry."

"No, I wasn't after an apology. Just concerned about you."

"I'm fine." The words were a lie, but there was no way she was going to open up to Elise about the night before. They were work friends, and often supported each other with issues related to their teaching and their pupils, but they'd never really touched on private lives, and Bethany was happy to keep it that way.

"Well, if there's anything I can help with, just let me know."

"I will. Thanks."

No, she knew who could help, and as soon as her lunchtime shift was over, she nipped back to the staffroom to make a call.

That evening, when she arrived at her mum's house, Alice had already popped a quiche in the oven and thrown together a large mixed salad in a bowl. Two plates faced each other on the dining table, a jug of water with glasses sitting off to one side.

"So," Alice said, easing into one of the rickety chairs that ringed her table, "tell me all about it." She poured them each a glass of water and motioned Bethany into the chair opposite.

Bethany sat and huffed out a long breath. "I had a date with that Sarah woman last night."

"Oh! How was it?"

"Ugh."

"Oh." Alice sipped some water. "Explain 'ugh'."

"She's infuriating!" Bethany's voice was louder than she'd anticipated, and she smiled ruefully when her mum winced. "Sorry. She just...ugh, she confuses me and annoys me and yet she's so gorgeous and interesting and..."

"Bethany, love, any chance you could start at the beginning?"

Laughing, Bethany flopped back in her chair. "Okay, okay." She took a deep breath, then pieced together the events of the night before into a coherent tale that gave her mum all the salient points, ending with, "And then she tried to apologise and claim she was trying to be different with me, whatever that means, but I knew it was all rubbish so I left."

She sat back, arms folded across her chest.

Alice stared at her, gaze dropping to Bethany's folded arms and back up to meet her eyes. "I'm not sure you really believe it was all rubbish, as you say," she said, just as the oven timer pinged to report that the quiche was ready.

She stood and walked to the oven, Bethany staring at her as she did so.

"What do you mean?" she asked, indignant. Alice took her time responding, which only raised Bethany's ire further. "Mum?" she prompted impatiently.

"Well," Alice said as she returned to the table with the tray of quiche held in thick oven gloves. "If you really believed it was rubbish, I don't think you'd be in my kitchen right now wanting to talk all about it." She smirked as she sat down and removed her oven gloves, tossing them onto a spare chair. "If everything was as cut and dried as you claim, I wouldn't have got a phone call at lunchtime asking me if I was free this evening for a chat about 'something that's bothering me', would I?"

"All right, smarty pants," Bethany muttered, and Alice laughed.

Alice cut them each a generous slice of quiche and Bethany loaded up her own plate with a mountain of salad. They ate in silence, her mum waiting her out while Bethany thought through how to respond.

"She confused me," Bethany confessed eventually. "I wanted her to be the nice Sarah that helped me in the shop, the one that asked such good questions about my career last night, the one who's travelled a lot and loves wine and…"

"And she *was* all those things, wasn't she?"

Bethany nodded, then sighed, dropping her cutlery onto her half-empty plate. "She was. And so gorgeous, Mum. God…" She swallowed. "And then there were those total…asshole moments that made all of that seem to, I don't know, disappear."

"You don't think you were too hard on her, not staying when she apologised?"

"I didn't at the time." Bethany blushed. "But in the cold light of day, I do now."

"Are you going to call her? Talk to her?"

Bethany pondered that for a few moments. Could she? Did she want to? What if she did and Sarah either didn't want to talk to her, or turned out to be as shallow as some of those comments suggested? She didn't know which was the real Sarah—that was the trouble. Of course, the only way to find that out was to try to see her again…

"I don't know, Mum. I really don't know."

"Cheeky little sherry before dinner, Sarah?" Jonathan called from across the room.

"Of course," Sarah said with a grin.

They settled on the sofa with their drinks; Evelyn was already in her chair, her own glass of sherry on the small side-table next to her.

"So," Jonathan said, setting his drink down on the coffee table, "Evelyn tells me you have woman trouble."

"Yes," Evelyn chimed in, "why don't we get right on with it."

Sarah swallowed. Now that she was here with her requested audience, talking about it seemed stupid.

"Sure you don't want to eat first?"

"No," chorused two voices.

"Right. Okay." She took a deep breath. "Well, remember I mentioned that woman I met on Friday night?"

"The one who turned you down?" Jonathan clarified.

"Yeah. Her. Bethany. Well, I did give her my card before we parted ways, and she actually called me up yesterday, and we went out for drinks."

"Marvellous," Evelyn said, her eyes sparkling.

"It was. It was…wonderful. Um, mostly." Sarah shook her head in frustration.

"Wait." Jonathan held up a hand. "I'll get back to the 'mostly' comment in a second, but Sarah, did you just hear yourself then? How…dreamy you sounded?"

He was smirking. Sarah groaned.

"Yes. And that's part of the problem. She's made me weird."

Jonathan howled with laughter.

"Sarah, dear, what do you mean? Weird?" Evelyn looked perturbed.

Sarah shrugged. "You know… Weird. Like…like I didn't automatically just want a one-night stand with her. We talked and laughed, and we had a lot of interesting things in common. She's very sweet, a little shy, but she's also got this feisty streak to her. She knows what she wants." She chuckled. "And she was pretty amazing considering one of my, um, conquests from earlier this year tried to sabotage our evening." She shook her head. "I loved spending time with her and I realised I didn't need or want to play any of my usual games, not with her."

She glared at Jonathan, who was now chuckling into his sherry.

"Will you stop that? It's not funny."

"Oh, darling, it's perfect! Finally, *finally* you've found a woman to tame you." He stopped laughing and his eyes softened. "I'm very happy for you."

"Whatever," Sarah mumbled.

"Now, can we step back to the 'mostly' comment—what does that mean?"

His intense gaze made Sarah squirm. "Uh, well, I might have, um, said a few things I shouldn't," she offered meekly.

Jonathan rolled his eyes. "Oh, really." His tone was as dry as a desert. "Were you an asshole?"

"Jonathan!" Evelyn snapped.

"No, it's okay, Evelyn. He used the right word."

"Well, what does it mean?" Evelyn asked, looking confused.

Sarah sighed. "It means I was crass and immature and, well, 'a Neanderthal', as Bethany put it."

Jonathan snorted. "She actually called you that?"

"Yep."

"I like her," he said, grinning.

Sarah threw him a glare, but he merely laughed in her face.

"Well, I think she sounds awfully rude, dear." Evelyn's tone was haughty. "And," she said, waving a thin hand in the air, "now you know she is like that, you can move on. Your next adventure awaits." She smiled, her eyes bright.

"I guess," Sarah mumbled before she could stop herself. "She doesn't want to see me again anyway. She made that perfectly clear."

"Well, there you are then. Move on, dear." Evelyn sat back in her chair, satisfaction written all over her face.

"Whoa, wait up there, madam. I'm not sure that's what Sarah wants. Is it?" Jonathan stared at her.

Sarah blinked, swallowed, and opened her mouth to speak, but no words came out.

"Ah!" Jonathan exclaimed, triumphant.

"Now wait just a minute," Sarah said finally, sitting up straight, a mild panic coursing through her veins. "This is not a good thing. It's wrong, in so many ways. I can't do this."

"It's just not your style, is it, dear?" Evelyn sounded smug.

"Exactly! Thank you, Evelyn."

"Well, that's that sorted. Shall we have dinner?" Evelyn braced herself to rise from her chair.

"Hang on," Jonathan exclaimed, holding up a hand, "we're not remotely done here. Sarah, what exactly is your problem with this situation?"

Evelyn sat back down, sighing.

Sarah knew it was a long shot thinking she'd be able to get away without a Jonathan lecture. "I dunno."

Voice like acid, Jonathan said, "Sarah, you are thirty-two years old, not fourteen. I am quite certain you can express yourself more eloquently than that."

She took a few moments to find the words. Talking about feelings had never been her strong point.

"I feel unsettled by last night. Apart from the bits I screwed up, the evening was wonderful and yet so very far from my comfort zone. Being with Bethany made me feel things I've never felt before, and I don't know what to do about that." She closed her eyes. "It scares me," she finished, her voice only just above a whisper.

For once, both Evelyn and Jonathan were silent.

Then Jonathan said, "And what exactly scares you?"

"Feeling," Sarah replied, still whispering. "Caring. Trusting." She looked up at Evelyn. "I can't help thinking back to Amber."

Evelyn nodded, a small frown on her face. "I understand. I mean, it is rather different circumstances, but, yes, I can see why you would think that." She pressed her hands together. "If you are not ready, you are not ready. I say, don't worry about it, and move on. There is nothing that says you have to settle down yet. You are only thirty-two, Sarah. You should be out enjoying yourself, not worrying about all that serious business."

"Who's Amber?" Jonathan turned to look at Sarah.

Sarah waved the question off. "Thanks, Evelyn. You're right."

"Wait, who's Amber?" Jonathan's face was creased into a deep frown. "And who says Evelyn's right?"

"Of course I am right!" Evelyn said, sitting up in her chair and crossing her arms.

"I don't think she is at all, Sarah," Jonathan said, his tone beseeching, "and I don't think you really want to do all this playing around anymore either. I think meeting Bethany has made that very clear to you."

"Argh!" Sarah stood up and paced the room. "I knew it was a mistake talking to you two."

"Sarah." Jonathan spoke softly, as if afraid she'd run out of the room if he pushed any harder. "Who's Amber?"

Sarah stopped pacing and turned away, leaning against the mantelpiece and closing her eyes.

"Tell him, dear. Then he will understand. And then perhaps we will be able to eat." Evelyn's tone was scathing, and Sarah couldn't help snorting.

She turned back to face Jonathan, who was topping off their sherry glasses.

"Are you trying to get me drunk?" Evelyn snapped, although she did reach for the filled glass.

"Anything to shut you up, Evelyn dear," Jonathan said with a wink.

Evelyn tutted, but her eyes were twinkling as she sipped her sherry.

Sarah took the glass Jonathan offered her, sipping once before speaking.

"Amber was my best friend from about the age of fourteen. We were so close, did everything together, and she helped me a lot when all that stuff came out about my family. I always knew there was something different about me, and I finally got comfortable with my sexuality when I was about seventeen, so it made perfect sense to tell my best friend, right?" Sarah sighed. "But Amber never gave me a chance to explain that I wasn't coming out to her because I fancied her. I just wanted my closest friend to know this one important, but at the same time irrelevant, thing about me, but she completely misconstrued it."

"Oh, shit," Jonathan murmured.

"Quite," Evelyn said.

"Yeah." Sarah sat back down on the sofa next to Jonathan and took another sip. "So, Amber ran, and refused to return any of my calls or emails. When I tried to see her at her parents' house, her mother turned me away, a nasty sneer on her face. And that was the end of that."

When she looked at Jonathan, the sympathetic understanding was clear on his face.

"The whole thing blew what little trust I had in people out the water. After what happened with my parents, and the way she'd stood by me, and been there for me, I trusted Amber with my true self. And she threw that back in my face." She gulped down the last of her drink. "So, I can't do that again. I can't let anyone get that close."

The tears were forming but there was no way she was going to let them fall. She swallowed hard a few times until the urge to cry went away.

"Oh, Sarah," Jonathan said, one hand slowly reaching for hers and squeezing tight. "Thank you for telling me that. But..." He sighed. "Bethany is not Amber. For one thing, Bethany appears to be completely at ease with her own sexual orientation. For another, she is a mature adult, and everything you've told us about last night makes it sound like she's a lovely person."

Sarah met Jonathan's eyes. "I know," she whispered.

Much to her surprise, his words tempered the pain that always accompanied the retelling of the Amber story. Even Evelyn, to some extent, had tried to dissuade her from being so distrustful of everyone after Amber, but she had refused to listen. As a consequence, over the years she had gradually descended into a life of meaningless hook-ups and way too much partying. And it was Evelyn who had come down hard on her in her mid-twenties when Sarah's drinking had threatened to get out of control. It was why she had turned to exercise, healthy eating, and drinking alcohol only in moderation.

Jonathan had come into Evelyn's life in the midst of Sarah's wilder years, and had watched—and helped—her progression to the healthy woman she was now. He gazed at her with love, affection, and understanding.

"You like Bethany, yes?"

Sarah nodded. That was most definitely true. She smiled as an image of Bethany's face appeared in her mind's eye.

"Then why fight it? Why not try, just this once, to see how different it can be to have a real relationship, rather than a one-night stand?"

"Relationship?" Sarah squeaked, her eyebrows shooting upwards.

Jonathan chuckled. "Yes, darling. Relationship. Go on a second date. And a third. And here's a thought—don't have sex with her until she makes it very clear she's ready. And when you do, don't do your usual and sneak away from her the next morning. Try cuddling. And breakfast in bed. See where it takes you, rather than letting it scare you away."

That was crazy, but at the same time, with Bethany in mind, it all sounded…tempting.

"But what if she won't see me again?"

Jonathan shrugged. "You won't know unless you ask her."

"Evelyn, what do you think?" Sarah asked.

Her aunt shrugged. "You know what I think, dear. There is so much time to have a relationship later. You can have lots of fun now and still think about that in the future."

Jonathan snorted. "Why am I not surprised that's your response?"

Evelyn huffed. "I am entitled to my opinion, you know."

"True," Jonathan concurred. "And one day you'll tell me just why you are so averse to anyone settling down. But," he turned to look directly at her, "it's your choice, Sarah. Your aunt and I clearly have different ideas about what you should do with your life, but it is *your* life. Your choice."

Sarah slumped back against the sofa.

"Yeah, I know. Thanks." She smiled at them both. "I mean it. Thanks for listening and everything."

They both nodded.

"Can we eat now?" Evelyn asked.

CHAPTER 7

"I'M SORRY, BUT THAT'S ALL Professor Mitchell has time for," the seminar host said, and Bethany dropped her hand. Her question would have to remain unanswered, but perhaps, as the professor had said, she could email it through.

"I'd like to thank Professor Mitchell for her time this evening, and I'm sure you'll all agree that it was, indeed, illuminating research which gives us much to think about." The host began clapping and the room joined her in a long round of applause. Professor Mitchell nodded numerous times until the clapping gradually came to a halt and the room filled instead with the murmur of many voices and chairs pushing back.

Bethany bent to pick up her shoulder bag, stuffing the seminar notes and her notebook into its depths before slinging its long strap over her head to drop down over one shoulder. With the bag securely nestled on one hip, she walked along the now empty row of chairs to the aisle.

"Bethany? Oh, wow, is that really you?"

She knew the voice, and in the split second it took to register in her brain, she threw a huge sigh at the universe. *Really? Her? After all this time? Thanks a bunch.* Bethany turned to her left, to the row of chairs opposite the one she'd just left, schooling her features as she'd done so many times in the past when faced with—

"Jessica." Bethany swallowed and smiled, forcing the shape of it onto her mouth and praying she wouldn't make a fool of herself in the next however many minutes Jessica's presence would torture her.

Jessica Rogers, Bethany's long-time crush from teacher training, was standing a few feet away, eyes wide, head shaking as she grinned. She looked, of course, amazing. Her dark brown hair was longer, her face a little fuller, but she still had that...*something* that had tugged at Bethany all through college. Jessica had been a year ahead of Bethany, and whether it was because of that, or simply because of who she was, she'd always gone about life with an air of confidence and poise that had left Bethany both envious and breathless.

Jessica stepped closer and opened her arms.

A hug? Seriously? Oh, God. In all the time she'd crushed on Jessica, she'd barely even spoken to her, and had never had anything like physical contact with her. The thought of Jessica's arms wrapping around her now almost had her hyperventilating.

Bethany wanted to back away, but it would have been rude, so she stepped in, heart pounding, aiming to keep their contact to a minimum lest she combust. She held her breath and held Jessica loosely, scared to feel that body against hers. Scared of what she might do if she held on too long. Jessica's perfume filled her nostrils, something light and fruity, and she bit back a moan as Jessica's arms pressed into her back and shoulders as she squeezed.

"Gosh, it's been years, hasn't it?" Jessica observed as she pulled back from the hug. "How are you?"

Shaking, and trying hard not to show it, Bethany replied, "I'm well. And you?" *How can you still look so...everything?*

"Marvellous. Life is good."

"That's great. Just...great."

"I take it you're still teaching, then, given you're here?" Jessica grinned.

"Oh, yes. Primary school. In Finchley." Okay, two-word sentences weren't the most eloquent, but given how disconcerting it was to actually talk to Jessica, it was the best she could hope for in the moment. She really did look amazing, and Bethany's body was warm all over at the sight of Jessica talking to her and smiling at her.

"Oh, lovely! I am too, but Years seven to nine. It's...challenging," Jessica replied with a laugh.

Oh, that laugh. It was mesmerising how it transformed Jessica's face— one minute serenely beautiful, the next, open and bright, and...stunning.

Bethany swallowed hard; even two-word sentences had abandoned her.

"So, what did you think of the seminar?" Jessica asked, reaching out to tug Bethany to one side of the aisle as a group of loudly chatting women marched past.

Her hand was warm on Bethany's arm, just below where her three-quarter sleeve ended. Much to Bethany's surprise, she didn't burst into flames at the touch.

"It was"—her voice croaked, and she cleared it loudly—"very interesting."

Inwardly, she groaned. *Oh yes, you sound incredibly intelligent, Bethany. Jessica will be so impressed with that erudite summing up of the presentation.*

Jessica smiled. "Yes, it was." She glanced down at her watch. "And I would love to talk more about it with you, but damn, I have to be somewhere else." She looked back up at Bethany. "You know," she mused, one finger tapping at her chin, "we should meet up. Catch up on old times. I always wondered what happened to you."

Bethany opened her mouth to speak but no words were forthcoming. Jessica had thought about *her*? She hadn't realised Jessica even knew who she was. Bethany had been perpetually shy whenever their paths had crossed, her crush reducing her to a silent, quivering mess in Jessica's mere presence.

"Um, sure," she found herself responding. "We could get a drink sometime?"

You just asked Jessica Rogers out for a drink. Who are you and what have you done with your real self?

Well, she was supposed to be doing this dating thing again, so why the hell not carry on the quest with the biggest crush of her life?

She almost snorted out loud.

Jessica blushed. Actually, really blushed.

"I'd like that." Her voice was soft, her eyes wide. "I know it's probably short notice, but are you free next Tuesday or Wednesday?"

Bethany knew she had no plans for the following week but made a show of pretending to consult a mental calendar so it didn't look too desperate when she said, "Wednesday would be fine. Where would you like to meet?"

"Well, I work in Islington, near Angel, and I know there's lots of great pubs and bars around there. Shall we meet by the Tube at, say, seven?"

"Yes, that sounds easy. Great." *A date with Jessica. Holy moly.*

"Here, let me give you my number, just in case, um, something crops up and, you know, you can't make it."

Jessica was stuttering, all the poise Bethany remembered her possessing seeming to have deserted her. She seemed…nervous, and that was confusing the heck out of Bethany.

They swapped numbers, then stood staring at each other for a few moments.

"Well, it…it was super to see you again," Jessica gushed, the pink returning to her pale cheeks.

"Yes, it was." Bethany genuinely smiled for the first time since they'd bumped into each other.

"See you Wednesday." Jessica gave her a dinky wave that seemed so incongruous for the cool woman who had left Bethany weak at the knees for such a long time.

As Jessica headed for the door, Bethany shook her head. *Who would have thought…?*

She watched Jessica go, noting the sway of her hips in the tight black jeans she wore, the bounce of her hair on her shoulders, the perfect way she managed to walk in heels without a single stumble. Beautiful. Her body trembling, Bethany tore her gaze away from Jessica's retreating back and sucked in a big breath.

I'm having a drink with her next week. Yikes.

Maybe I should just cancel tonight. Bethany stared at her reflection in the mirror and sighed. But this was *Jessica.* She sighed again.

Being back in the dating world was putting Bethany's head in a spin. Sarah hadn't left her mind, and she was still debating whether to call and give her that second chance. After talking it through with her mum, she'd promised she would consider it, but work and Netflix had provided easy distractions from actually doing the considering, and now, of all things, there was Jessica.

She groaned and flopped back onto the bed.

Sarah was gorgeous, and funny, and interesting. But clearly a player who was used to women falling into her bed after she delivered those cheesy, macho lines. She was also someone who seemed to respect that Bethany didn't want to see her, as she hadn't made any attempt to get in contact. Or was it more that she'd realised she wasn't going to get what she wanted with Bethany—an uncomplicated one-night stand—and had already moved on to another Kristen?

The thought left Bethany cold, and she shifted her thinking to Jessica, the woman of her dreams. A woman Bethany actually didn't know much about. So it would be stupid to write Jessica off before she'd even been out with her, wouldn't it? And particularly stupid if Bethany still had doubts about the type of person Sarah was, and whether they could have a chance of something.

Bethany threw her arms up above her head and puffed out a breath.

Okay, you have a date—or something—with Jessica in a little over an hour, and you are sitting here thinking about Sarah. Not good.

Hauling herself upright, she stared into her open wardrobe, agonising over what to wear. She was woefully unprepared for being suddenly thrust back into the dating limelight. Dates were, apparently, like London buses—you wait eight years for one, and two come along at once. Her gaze swept over every item on every hanger and back again before a decision was made. Cute cropped jeans, red sneakers, and a summery jumper of cream cotton with three-quarter sleeves.

Once she was dressed, she felt better; a little zip of excitement ran through her at the thought of spending time with her old crush. Yet it still felt unreal too, and she'd have to try hard to not let her old stumbling self take hold in Jessica's presence.

The Tube to Angel only took twenty minutes, which meant she was early by about ten. Even so, Jessica was waiting for her in the ticket hall, and Bethany's stomach did an excited back flip at the sight of her.

Jessica's smile was wide, and her hug of greeting warm. Bethany allowed herself a few seconds in the embrace, and almost shook her head in amazement. *I'm hugging Jessica Rogers!*

"Hello," Bethany said when they pulled apart, smiling as best she could despite the trembling in her limbs.

"Hi. I'm so glad you came." Jessica shuffled from foot to foot, her hands clasped tight around the strap of her over-the-shoulder handbag. She looked good; her dress was emerald green, with a wide neckline that showed off fabulous collar bones and a smooth line of neck that Bethany could barely tear her gaze away from. "You look great," Jessica said, a faint blush on her cheeks.

"So do you. I love this dress."

Jessica dipped her head as she murmured, "Thank you," and then gestured towards the exit. "Shall we?"

The bar she led them to was only about five minutes' walk from the Tube, and while busy, wasn't heaving or too loud. They each ordered a glass of wine and found a small table near the door which led to the smoking courtyard at the back.

"Is this okay?" Jessica asked. "I'm worried it will get smoky near here, so we can move if—"

"It's fine, Jessica. Really."

Jessica's lack of poise was disconcerting. It was hard to reconcile this version of her with the one Bethany had held in her mind all these years. It was endearing on the one hand, and sort of...disappointing on the other. She brushed off the thought. This was still Jessica Rogers.

"Okay." Jessica's stiff posture eased, and she leaned back in her chair. "Okay, good." She smiled brightly. "So, how was your weekend?"

"Um, it was good. I spent some time with my mum, did some baking." *Did that sound lame?*

"Sounds lovely." Jessica seemed genuine, which made Bethany breathe a little easier.

"What about you?"

"Oh, the usual. Marking, lesson planning, making sure I was up to date with my continual development. Hosted a workshop with some colleagues on recognising the signs of bullying. It's an initiative I feel strongly about and have become somewhat of an expert in."

There was a hint of boastfulness in that last statement that didn't sit well with Bethany, but she decided to push it aside.

"Wow, that's pretty much a working weekend, then," she said. "No free time?" She sipped her wine, grateful for the warm buzz it was already inducing in her.

Jessica laughed. "I forget what free time is. It's one of the reasons I've had so little time for dating these past couple of years."

Even Bethany, far removed from the dating game, recognised that statement for what it was: Jessica making it clear she was single.

She smiled. "No other half waiting for you at home, then?" It was bold, and possibly flirtatious—she had no idea, really—but she wanted to make sure that was where this was going.

Jessica raised her eyebrows. "Well, no. I...I wouldn't have suggested we meet if there was."

"Oh." Bethany broke out into a sweat. *Okay, so this is definitely a date.*

Before she could pursue the subject, Jessica frowned and said, "Do *you* have someone waiting at home?"

"No! Definitely not. I'm only just getting back into dating myself. So, no. Definitely no."

"Okay. Well, that's...good." Jessica's frown deepened. "So does that mean you are currently dating someone, even if just, you know, casually?"

Oh God, she was like a terrier with a chew toy, but Bethany couldn't lie.

"Not exactly, but I'll be honest, I did go on a date last weekend."

"Oh, really?" Something twitched just above Jessica's left eyebrow. "Was she nice?"

"Um, yes. It was...nice."

"Nice?"

"Er, yes." Bethany sighed. *This isn't weird. Not at all.*

"Will you see her again?" Jessica was now pushed so far back in her chair that she was practically in the courtyard, and Bethany didn't quite know what to make of the change in body language.

"Maybe. No. Ugh, I don't know."

Jessica sipped her wine, then put her glass down with a sense of purpose that instantly put Bethany on alert.

"Bethany, can I ask you something?"

She nodded, then waited.

Jessica's fingers played with the stem of her wine glass. "Why...why did you arrange this date with me if you were already dating someone else?" The words came out in a rush, and Jessica glanced once at Bethany before dipping her head.

"I-I didn't know if this was a date. And my date with her was probably... well, more than likely, a one-time thing, and happened long before I bumped into you on Thursday night. So..."

Jessica lifted her head and stared at Bethany. "You didn't know this was a date?" she asked quietly.

Bethany shook her head.

Smiling, Jessica also shook her head. "I'm sorry. I'm not very good at this, clearly. Out of practice," she mused. "Yes, I meant this to be a date. I was so excited to see you again after all this time. I…I always wanted to ask you out in college, but you were so unapproachable. I… Well, I assumed you just weren't that interested in me."

Bethany didn't know whether to laugh or cry, but her body decided on the former, the chuckle starting low in her chest and blossoming into a full-blown laugh.

"Oh, lordy," she said, gazing into Jessica's confused face. "I had such a crush on you in college that I couldn't go near you for fear I'd make a complete fool of myself."

"Y-you did?" Jessica was wide-eyed.

Bethany nodded.

"Wow," Jessica said, reaching for her wine with a trembling hand and gulping down a mouthful.

"Indeed," Bethany replied, swigging some of her own wine and contemplating the revelations of the last two minutes. She couldn't get used to this shy and nervous Jessica, but it warmed her that she'd been on Jessica's radar way back when.

"Well," Jessica said after a moment, "shall we start again?"

Bethany tilted her head. "What do you mean?"

Jessica smiled. "Hi, I'm Jessica. We met in college. I'd really like to go on a date with you."

Laughing, Bethany leaned forward in her chair. "Hi, Jessica. Yes, I remember you, and I'd really like to go on a date with you too."

They clinked glasses and sipped.

"So, tell me all about you," Jessica said, looking distinctly more relaxed. "Where do you work?"

The next hour passed in a blur. They filled in the blanks since college, talking about jobs, post-grad studies, classmates, and teachers. They ordered a second round, and when Jessica excused herself to the ladies' room, Bethany sat back in her chair and pondered how the evening was progressing.

It was nice. It was great to catch up, and to hear stories of people from college with whom each of them still had contact. But it was weird, because that was all they'd talked about. There'd been no easy segue into conversations about food, or wine, or travel—all the things she and Sarah had discussed—and that was sort of…boring.

Well, that's what we'll discuss next. When she gets back from the loo, I'll change the subject.

"So," she began once Jessica had sat down again, "have you done any travelling since college?"

Jessica chuckled. "Oh, yes, I've had some lovely trips with the school. We did a wonderful visit to the Peak District a couple of years ago, and of course the Eden Project the year before that. Next year we're hoping to take one class to Scotland, do Edinburgh and the Highlands."

"No, I mean, travel for you. You know, holidays, weekends abroad, that sort of thing."

"Oh! Oh, no. Not my thing. I'm happy being at home. I have two cats that I adore, and I can't leave them for long periods of time."

"Oh. Right." Bethany cleared her throat, and tried hard to tamp down the disappointment that churned in her gut. "Well, I travel a bit. Not as much as I'd like on our salary, of course, but…"

"Well, yes, obviously. Did you hear about the latest moves by the NUT in that regard?"

And she was off again, talking about school-related issues. Inwardly, Bethany sighed. This was proving far more difficult than she would have imagined. Jessica was surprisingly one-sided so far. Outside she glowed, and Bethany had noticed more than one head turn as she'd walked back from the loo, but inside it seemed things were slightly less shiny.

Maybe it's just nerves. Maybe I haven't found another topic that she can enthuse about yet.

"Gosh, sorry, I have rambled on a bit there about union business, haven't I?" Jessica's voice cut into Bethany's thoughts and she narrowly avoided starting.

"No, not at all. You're obviously very passionate about teaching and all it entails." *Did that sound sincere?*

Jessica smiled. "I am." She reached across the table and laid her hand on Bethany's. "It's lovely to finally meet someone who understands that."

There was warmth in the touch, of course, and something almost illicitly thrilling at being touched by the woman she'd admired from afar for so long. But it didn't send any little jolts of electricity up Bethany's arm, or cause her stomach to flutter. None of the things she'd expected that being touched by Jessica would do to her, after fantasising about her all that time.

"So, um, what hobbies do you have?"

Jessica pursed her lips and was silent for a few moments. "Well, I like reading."

"Oh, me too! What sort of books?"

"Well, mostly educational. I'm always on the lookout for new recommended practices, and, of course, reading the latest developments in the subjects I teach. One can't fall too far behind."

"No," Bethany murmured, and her heart sank a little. "No fiction?"

Jessica shrugged. "Sometimes. The odd bit of crime here and there."

"Oh, I like crime too. Not the very gory stuff, but more detective-type thrillers."

Jessica grinned. "Yes, same here. Have you read the Claire McNab ones from way back?"

"I have! All of them. And Andrea Bramhall and Cari Hunter are my other two favourites."

"Oh yes, I've read both of them too."

Jessica's eyes were bright as she launched into a detailed comparison of her favourites. Bethany chimed in with her own thoughts, and the rest of the pub faded into the background as they conversed, their hands active as they both spoke with passion about this shared interest. Bethany's hopes rose once again. So Jessica was very committed to her work—that was a good thing, right? Now that they were off on another subject they could both enjoy, it was easy to forget the earlier sense of being let down or bored.

This was okay. More than okay, really, because Jessica was smiling at her, and her hair was shining in the glow from the wall lights above her, and she was reaching across the table to tentatively nudge her fingers against Bethany's on the pitted and scarred wood.

"I hate to break up the evening," Jessica said, her voice soft, but as she was leaning in close, Bethany had no trouble hearing her. "But it is a school night, and I need to get my eight hours or I'll be fit for nothing tomorrow."

Bethany blinked, the mellow reverie of their conversation fading as Jessica's words registered.

"Oh, yes, of course!" She looked over at Jessica's watch. It was eight thirty. "No problem."

Jessica took her hand, holding it lightly, her thumb stroking across the knuckles. "I've had a lovely evening, Bethany," she said, her gaze locked on Bethany's.

"Me too." *Mostly*, a little voice added, and she banished it to the back of her mind.

"Can we...do this again? Soon?"

"Yes, I'd like that." *At least, I think I would. Why am I not sure?*

"Are you free next Tuesday? I'm afraid I'm busy with school business all weekend, but maybe we could go for dinner next week, not just drinks?"

Another weekend focused on the school?

"Dinner sounds good."

Despite her doubts, Bethany felt a little shiver of excitement at the thought of dinner with Jessica. A second date.

Jessica smiled. "Thank you. How about if we meet at the same time at Angel again? I know a lovely Lebanese place we could try?"

"Sounds wonderful."

Jessica let go of Bethany's hand, and although she missed the warmth, the letting go highlighted the fact that she hadn't really *noticed* Jessica holding her hand. Nothing about her touch had really registered other than that it was warm. Which was...odd.

They stood, grabbed their handbags, and Jessica led them out, past more admiring glances from the male population of the bar. Outside in the cool evening air, they both rubbed their arms and chuckled.

"Should have brought a cardigan," Jessica said. "At least you're in a jumper."

Bethany shrugged. "It's not as warm as it looks."

Jessica glanced up the street. "So, I'm heading to that bus stop."

"Oh, okay. Well, I'll head back to the Tube."

There was a moment's pause, then Jessica stepped in, leaned forward, and placed a gentle kiss on Bethany's cheek.

"I had a lovely time," she murmured as she pulled back, her eyes dark as they locked onto Bethany's.

"Me too."

"Bye." She gave that little wave again.

"Bye."

Jessica walked away, and Bethany turned to head to the station. As she walked along the busy road, people weaving around her from all sides, she tried hard to tell herself that the kiss had affected her, that it had made her tremble and wonder what would happen if—when—Jessica kissed her lips. The kiss had to do those things to her, because it was Jessica Rogers, the woman of her dreams, the woman she'd lusted after for *years*.

So why the heck *hadn't* it done a thing for her?

CHAPTER 8

"So," ALICE SAID, AND BETHANY could picture her settling into her sofa for the call, "how was your date with Jessica? And did you call Sarah again in the end? I can't believe how much I've missed in just one week away!"

Alice had just returned from a hastily-arranged—and much-needed—holiday in Spain with a couple of friends, and although she and Bethany had texted a couple of times, she was clearly keen to get a lot more detail on all the ins and outs of Bethany's love life given that she'd called the minute she arrived back home.

Bethany sighed and snuggled back into one of the few spots in her sofa that didn't dig into her backside. "Well, the short answer to those questions, in order, is fine and no."

"Oh. Well, I'll confess I'm a little surprised you didn't call Sarah, but you know what's best for you."

Do I? Bethany still wasn't sure it was the right decision, especially after the evening with Jessica.

"Okay, so tell me about Jessica. I couldn't believe it when you told me she was at that seminar. Must have been so strange being out on a date with someone you hadn't seen in such a long time."

Bethany told her mum all about it, explaining how it had felt, and trying hard to avoid comparisons with Sarah, but knowing she really wasn't succeeding.

"So, if I've got this right, Jessica was lovely but not hugely exciting, and you're seeing her again tomorrow. And Sarah was, um, interesting and more than exciting, but you've never called her back and she's never called you? Is that it?"

"Succinctly put, Mum," Bethany said, and groaned. "I keep thinking I really need to give this thing with Jessica a chance. I mean, it's *her*. I lost so much sleep over her back in college. I'd be insane not to try to get to the bottom of whatever it is we're starting."

"But...?"

"But despite not calling Sarah, I can't stop thinking about her. Of course, she hasn't called me either, so that tells me a lot." She sighed. "I know I expressed reservations about her lifestyle, for want of a better word, but then she assured me that it wasn't what she wanted from me and you seem to think she was honest about that, and I'm all confused every time I think about it." Her words were racing away with themselves. "And now the fact that she hasn't called makes me think that actually it *was* what she wanted from me, and because I didn't offer it to her on a plate, she's off to her next conquest. And if that's true, then I really don't want to know her, despite how bloody gorgeous she is." She huffed out a breath, and Alice's laughter rang in her ears.

"Oh dear. What a pickle you're in, love."

"I know."

God, what a pickle indeed. Bethany's sleep had been rubbish lately, with thoughts of both women tormenting her.

"Of course," Alice said, sounding serious, "you could just forget about the pair of them and find someone else. You're only just starting out again, love. You don't have to make any rash commitments, you know."

"I know. You're right." Bethany closed her eyes and sighed. "I've got a second date with Jessica tomorrow, and I'm not going to back out of that. That would just be rude. And if it doesn't, you know, blow me away, then I suppose I'll know."

"And Sarah?"

She hesitated. "I have no idea. Probably not."

It was painful saying it out loud, and with that came the almost certain knowledge that something important had been lost; missed out on. At the same time, her sense of self-preservation told her that keeping things easy and simple would lead to less heartbreak.

"I'm sorry, love. I'm proud of you for sticking to your guns on that one. A lot of women might have called her, and that would have probably only led to trouble."

"Aw, thanks, Mum."

"Well, like you said, you've got another date with Jessica. You can see how that goes, and then see how you feel."

"Yes." Bethany sat up straighter. Okay, she could do this. It wasn't the end of the world if things didn't make sense with Jessica, and who knew, maybe after their dinner they would, and she'd look back on this and laugh.

She and her mum chatted about other things for a few minutes, and then said their goodbyes.

"Remember, love, this is all about you. Be selfish. You need to make the right decisions for you, no one else, okay?"

"Thanks, Mum. I'll remember that."

"Night, love."

Bethany dropped the phone onto the sofa beside her and leaned her head back against the cushions. Her mum was right; she knew that. Bethany's brief relationship with Michelle, in that first year of college, had been a disaster because she'd compromised on everything. Now, more than ever, she knew she couldn't do that with the big things that mattered to her. Her integrity, for one thing—she deserved to be with someone who knew her value and appreciated her for who she was. And someone who gave her that spark, both mentally and physically; someone who made her laugh, and made her think, *and* made her go weak at the knees. She was entitled to it all, and she was going to get it.

She slapped her hands down on her thighs and said "Yes!" to the empty room before standing and heading to the bathroom to get ready for bed. It was early, but she'd take a book and read before she slept. Maybe something a little sexy, perhaps get herself in the mood to try the new vibrator out. Bizarrely, thanks to her nerves over the dates, she'd yet to use it, although she had gone as far as pulling it out of the box and washing it in preparation.

Chuckling, she stripped off her clothes and dumped them in the laundry basket, then wrapped herself in her silky summer robe before reaching for her toothbrush. As she brushed, she inspected herself in the mirror and liked what she saw; there was a determination in her eyes that looked good on her.

After retrieving her phone from the living room, she switched off all the lights on her way to the bedroom. She pulled back the duvet and sat on the bed, and was about to set the alarm on her phone when it rang. She gasped in surprise, nearly dropping it to the bed. After juggling it a couple of times, she managed to get it under control, just in time to see the caller ringing off.

Bugger. She swiped open the screen into her missed calls list and her heart jumped in her chest.

Sarah.

She waited a few moments to see if a voicemail notification appeared. Nope. So, now what did she do? Call back? Or was the call merely a case of mistaken dialling and therefore calling back would be a mistake? Did she want to call Sarah back? And if so, what did she want to say?

She knew it was a no-brainer. Now that Sarah had reached out, Bethany couldn't ignore her. Sitting back, pulling the duvet up to her chest, she exhaled a deep, long breath.

Okay.

Sarah answered on the first ring. "Bethany?"

"Hi, Sarah."

"I'm sorry," Sarah said in a rush. "For screwing up that date, and not calling you since, and—"

"It's okay," Bethany said, chuckling despite her doubts and confusion. Sarah in a panic was sort of endearing. "Breathe, please."

Sarah barked out a laugh, then sucked in a breath. "Sorry," she said again, her voice sounding sheepish. "I am normally better at this."

"What, talking?"

This time Sarah guffawed. "Um, yeah, that too." She sighed. "So, how are you? Is it too late to chat?"

Bethany leaned back against her pillow. She had no idea why Sarah was suddenly calling, but now that she had, Bethany wanted to hear her out. "No, not too late at all."

"Good. Good. So, um, how are you?"

"I'm fine. Working hard, of course." Should she? Yes—she'd been honest with Jessica, so Sarah should get the same treatment. "And I had an evening out with someone I knew from college. Well, a date, actually."

"Oh?" Sarah paused. "How...how was it?" Her voice shook, and that gave Bethany a thrill.

"It was nice. We're...well, we're going to see each other again tomorrow."

"Oh. Oh, well, I'll, um, I'll say goodbye then."

"Sarah, why didn't you call?" Bethany asked quickly, before she could hang up.

There was a long sigh. "I...I needed to get some stuff sorted. About me, and what I want, and how I want to change some things."

"And why did you call tonight?" Bethany had no idea where this strength was coming from, to ask the tricky questions, but it felt really good.

"I, um. Well, I was calling to see if you wanted to get together again. I meant what I said on our first date, Bethany—somehow with you I don't want to do the one-night stand thing. I would like..." She cleared her throat. "...to date you. To spend some time getting to know you." The intensity in her words sent goose bumps careering over Bethany's skin.

"Why? I mean, why me?" Her voice came out stronger than she'd dared hope; inside she was a quivering mess.

Sarah chuckled. "Because somehow, ever since I met you at the shop, I cannot get you out of my head. And that never happens to me, so I don't think I should waste that feeling."

"Oh." Bethany's entire body had turned to jelly.

"Look, I respect that you have another date with your college friend, but would there be any way we could spend some time together at the weekend?" Sarah's voice had dropped to that lower, husky tone she'd used a couple of times at the shop, but somehow Bethany knew it wasn't deliberate this time. It was simply the level of emotion coming through. And that made her tremble. "We don't have to call it a date," Sarah continued, "if that makes it easier. And if your date goes well tomorrow, you just let me know and we'll forget our plans. But if there's any way I could get a second chance with you, I'd really like to—"

"I'd love to. I'm free all weekend." Bethany slapped herself on the forehead. How bad did that sound?

"Really? Oh, that's great! Well," Sarah rushed on, "I was wondering about lunch on Saturday somewhere along the South Bank, perhaps Gabriel's Wharf?"

"That sounds lovely," Bethany said quietly. Was she capitulating too easily? Should she wait, and go on the second date with Jessica first before she made plans with Sarah? Could she really trust what Sarah was saying, about wanting to change? She decided she'd know for sure very soon, one way or another. Either she'd have had an amazing time with Jessica and want to pursue that, or she'd be really looking forward to spending time with Sarah because whatever was happening with Jessica wasn't going anywhere.

And if Sarah really was into one-night stands and nothing else, surely she wouldn't have suggested lunch, would she? Lunch meant saying goodbye before the evening got underway, so was that Sarah's way of showing that she wasn't expecting anything more from the day?

"Brilliant." Sarah sounded relieved now. "We could meet in front of the Festival Hall, if you like? Say, around one?"

"Perfect."

Don't get ahead of yourself. All of this planning could be for nothing if Jessica blows your mind tomorrow evening.

"Great!" Sarah sighed. "And Bethany, I meant what I said. If your date goes well, just message me to cancel." She chuckled. "I'm torn between wishing you well for that date—because if she's right for you then that's wonderful—and wanting you to have a crap time so you'll come out with me again." She sighed. "God, I can't believe I just said that out loud. Forgive me."

"You know," Bethany said, "there's nothing to forgive. I appreciate your honesty. And I won't lie to you, Jessica is someone I've liked for a long time, so I can't help but be hopeful about tomorrow."

"Ouch." Sarah's voice was soft.

"I know." Bethany closed her eyes and breathed out slowly. "But I really like you, Sarah, so if I'm totally honest, I'm torn too."

"Oh. Wow."

"I'd better go," Bethany said in a rush, as guilt over somehow betraying Jessica with that last statement flooded her. "I need to be up early."

"I understand." Sarah sighed. "Good luck for tomorrow, Bethany. I mean that."

"Thank you. I'll let you know about Saturday."

"Okay."

The line went silent and moments later the call disappeared from her phone's screen. Bethany dropped sideways onto the bed, groaning loudly.

How the heck is this fair, universe?

Sarah. How she'd sounded on the phone, kind of nervous and excited and…upset when she thought she might not see Bethany again. How she had looked in that red top last week, her deep brown eyes sparkling in the low light of the bar. How those eyes had stared deep into Bethany's and held her captive.

Bethany moaned; she was throbbing, and any thoughts of Jessica had fled. There was nothing but Sarah on her mind and stirring her blood. And she suddenly knew exactly what to do with the rest of her evening. Every inch of her skin was tingling in anticipation, enhanced by the feel of the silken material of her robe caressing her body with every move she made. She opened the drawer of the bedside cabinet and pulled the vibrator from where it lay nestled on the tissue paper its box had been wrapped in. She set it on the bed, her gaze never leaving it as she peeled off her robe and let it drop to the floor. Would it feel odd, maybe a bit alien to use something other than her own fingers? Only one way to find out.

She climbed back under the duvet, the small vibrator clutched in her right hand. Normally when masturbating, she'd take her time to get warmed up—caressing her breasts, her belly, and her thighs. Tonight that wouldn't be necessary; her clit was already responding to the excitement coursing through her, and there was a definite wetness between her legs.

One press of the soft silicone button that adjusted the settings and a gentle hum came from under the duvet. The vibrations running through her fingertips were steady and set an easy pace. She knew there were many other settings, but for a first time, this would do. Feeling slightly silly and quashing that thought as fast as it arose, she pushed the toy between her legs.

Oh my good God!

It was…exquisite. There was no other word for it.

She gasped and moaned as the buzz stimulated her clit in ways she wouldn't have imagined. Fantasies often played a role in her masturbation, and she didn't see why that should be any different now with a vibrator, so she started to imagine someone there with her. Usually the woman was rather faceless, merely a means by which Bethany could imagine breasts and wetness and excitement. But tonight, her mind was full of Sarah, and imagining what her body would be like sent Bethany's arousal soaring.

She arched her hips, picturing Sarah's fingers trailing exactly where the vibrator was, then swore as the toy tumbled from her fingers and bounced onto the mattress between her thighs. After a second or two of fumbling, she got it back in her hand and under control, and right back where it needed to be.

Oh yes. Just…there. Or maybe…there.

Oh, God.

Rubbing it up and down between her legs, she played with where the sensations felt the best. Before long she was panting, having found exactly the right spot, and her hips were undulating to their own rapid rhythm. Sarah was there, leaning down to kiss her, her fingers pushing inside Bethany and—

Her orgasm seemed to creep up on her out of nowhere, but when it found her, she could swear she saw stars.

Oh my Lord.

Breathing heavily, she flopped back down onto the bed, the toy still wedged between her legs where it hummed happily to itself.

And, of course, the humming still felt rather lovely, and if she just moved it—

Holy moly.

The second orgasm had her gasping for air. How was that possible—two orgasms in a couple of minutes? It seemed fantasising about a real, live woman she knew and was attracted to could work wonders.

And her body wasn't finished yet. She groaned as she slid the toy further down—she knew exactly what she needed now. It slipped inside her so easily, and the sensation of it pushing her open while it buzzed out its steady rhythm had her holding her breath in wonder.

She let her mind drift into some of her naughtiest fantasies, the ones that involved toys other than vibrators, the ones that delved into her deepest needs, and then came an image of Sarah pinned beneath her on the bed, her wrists tied to—

Bethany cried out, her eyes shut tight, her legs going rigid, the toy shooting out of her as her muscles spasmed. She laughed, and collapsed back onto the bed, wondrous sensations still pounding through her body.

Even as she sent a silent "thank you" to her imaginary Sarah, she winced with the guilty realisation that thoughts of Jessica, as beautiful as she was, didn't have nearly the same effect.

←——→

Sarah collapsed back on the sofa, her hand rubbing over her chest where her heart threatened to beat out of her ribs. That phone call was one of the most nerve-wracking things she'd ever done, and that admission made her shake her head in disbelief.

But, she'd done it, and although it hadn't gone quite as well as she would have liked, she had a second date—sort of—with Bethany this weekend. Well, a 'perhaps' date, if Bethany didn't end up falling in love with that Jessica woman. Whom she'd liked for ages.

Oh shit.

She grabbed her phone again and dialled Jonathan.

"Okay, I did it," she gushed when he answered. "But it didn't go that well and now I'm thinking I shouldn't have bothered."

"Huh?"

"I called Bethany! And I sort of have a second date with her on Saturday, but only if she doesn't fall in love with some other woman tomorrow night."

"Sarah, what the hell are you talking about? I mean, I'm proud of you for asking her out, but...?"

"Yeah, I know." She stood up quickly, pacing to work off the excess nervous energy. As she strode around her living room, she filled Jonathan in.

"Oh, I see," he said, once she was done. "Well, that's a little tricky."

"Tell me about it!"

"Although, I do admire the woman's gumption. She could have easily brushed you off, or spun you a yarn, but credit to her, she just came right out and told it how it was."

"Yeah, I was...well, I was kind of proud of her for doing that. For not bullshitting me."

"She's got integrity. I like her."

"Yeah, well, me too," Sarah mumbled, embarrassed to admit it. "And I guess we'll see what happens on Saturday."

"So, on the assumption she goes ahead with meeting you, where are you taking her?"

She outlined her lunch suggestion. "Should I have pushed the boat out for dinner instead? She seemed to like the lunch idea, and—"

"Saturday lunch is a wonderful idea—it sends a clear message that you have no expectations other than a casual meal to see how things are between you. Oh God, please tell me that's true?"

"It is!" Sarah was indignant, but she could understand why Jonathan asked. This was entirely not her style, after all. "Plus she already told me she doesn't have a lot of money, so I didn't want to take her to one of my usual upmarket restaurants where the prices would probably terrify her."

"That is extremely thoughtful of you, Sarah. Well done."

Sarah's blush deepened, but she was grinning. "Well, at the risk of sounding a bitch, let's hope her night with Jessica isn't all that great and I do get to take her on this casual lunch."

"And how would you feel if her date with the other woman *did* go well?"

Sarah stopped pacing and stared out the big windows into the dark night beyond. "Gutted," she whispered.

Jonathan sighed. "Well, I don't wish ill on anyone, you know me, but I can't help being on your side in this. Bring on the shit date for her and this other woman."

Sarah laughed, her shoulders relaxing. "You're terrible. But lovely."

"You know it."

She walked over to the doors and stepped out onto the deck to gaze down at the water below. "So, is Evelyn in bed?"

"Yes, went up about fifteen minutes ago."

"Okay. Give her my love in the morning."

"I will."

"Oh, and er, no need to share this snippet of news with her just yet. Let's see if, and how, the second date goes first."

Jonathan chuckled. "She's going to be very miffed at you."

"Why?"

"Well, if you take yourself off the singles market, where is she going get her fill of saucy gossip? God knows, she gets nothing from me."

"But that's your choice too, isn't it? I mean, I thought you hated the scene and all that sleeping around?"

"Oh, I do, definitely." He sighed. "I'm lonely, Sarah, that's all. I've been single now for two years, ever since Stefan moved to Australia. I want to be in love again. I want the romance, and the candlelit dinners, and the tickets to the opera."

"I thought you hated opera?"

"It's a metaphor, darling. You know what I mean—I want the whole romantic, seductive works."

Sarah swallowed. "Shit, is that what I need to do too? I mean, assuming I get past this second date with Bethany and want more, of course."

Jonathan snorted. "Sarah, I think we both know that is *definitely* what you want. So yes, you need to get in touch with your romantic soul. Do you have one lurking in that cold and bitter heart of yours somewhere?"

"Hey, no need for that! Bitch."

Jonathan's laughter rang out.

CHAPTER 9

JESSICA WAS, ONCE AGAIN, WAITING for Bethany when the escalator delivered her to the ticket hall at Angel station on Tuesday night. Bethany's stomach flipped at the gorgeous sight, and even though she'd been beset by doubts throughout the day and during the hour it had taken to get ready for this date, the sight of this beautiful woman smiling so widely at her did set her heart fluttering.

They hugged in greeting, and once again Jessica's light scent teased at Bethany's nose, conjuring up images of walks in the park on hot summer days, picnics by a lake or river, and afternoons curled up on a blanket together with a book. While romantic and lovely, those images did not contain anything like the passion she would have expected to feel for someone who had set her on fire, metaphorically speaking, when they were younger. And passion was something Bethany craved as much as all of those romantic ideals.

"You look amazing," Jessica whispered, stepping back to rake Bethany with an obviously appreciative gaze.

"Thank you." Bethany blushed under the attention. The dress she was wearing had been chosen days before and ironed to within an inch of its life. It was red, a colour Bethany needed a certain level of bravery to attempt, but she'd given herself pep talk after pep talk to ensure she would wear it with the confidence it deserved. The dress hugged her chest and hips, finishing just above her knees, and she'd matched it with low-heeled red shoes and a black handbag. She'd liked the look on herself, and had to admit that Jessica's wide-eyed stare and gentle blush were giving her quite the boost.

She took in Jessica's outfit and shook her head in admiration. The woman clearly knew how to dress her long-legged body to perfection. The grey dress trousers were slim-fitting, and tapered into her ankles to show off gorgeous turquoise heels that added at least two inches to her height. Her top was some sort of silky material in the same turquoise, and with her dark hair loose around her shoulders, the colour stood out even more.

"You look pretty wow yourself," Bethany said, smiling.

Jessica flicked her hair back with one hand, her expression a little… smug? Something squirmed in Bethany's stomach.

"Shall we?" Jessica gestured to the exit and Bethany fell into step alongside her.

"So, how has your week been?" she asked as they sidestepped a large group of young men who already seemed the worse for wear this early on a Tuesday evening.

"Very good. I've had an excellent week of teaching, some real successes with my anti-bullying initiative, and I'm feeling so positive about all the activities I have planned for the summer. How about you?"

Bethany wasn't sure how to respond. Her own accomplishments felt small fry compared to Jessica's, and she didn't want to share about the call with Sarah—not this time. She'd promised herself she would give this date with Jessica a real chance, and she didn't think mentioning Sarah in the middle of it would help.

"Um, good. Yes. No one threw up on me, at least." She chuckled but stopped after a moment when she realised Jessica wasn't laughing with her. Instead, she was frowning.

"Is that really something to celebrate? I mean," Jessica rushed on, "I can't imagine being so blasé about a child vomiting on me—and you're making that into a joke."

Bethany stared at her. She'd done the same training as Jessica, but it was as if they were from two entirely different professions.

"Well, yes. We all joke about it. It's just part of the territory with the young ones. Surely you've experienced it at some point in your career?"

Jessica grimaced. "Thankfully, no." She smiled then, but it lacked warmth. "Good for you to take it so…calmly."

This was not the best start to the evening Bethany could have imagined. It was almost as if Jessica was judging her for being so tolerant of the children in her care. She didn't understand—Jessica had been at the top of all of her classes, Bethany remembered, and she'd heard other trainees talking about her with awe. Maybe the reality of teaching full time had jaded her. Bethany could understand that; she loved her job, but there were days when she questioned why she'd wanted to do it in the first place.

A change of subject was needed, but before she could open her mouth, Jessica pointed across the road.

"That's the restaurant. I phoned earlier and booked a table."

The Lebanese place was tucked on a corner of the main road and a side street, and painted in garish colours that made Bethany smile.

"It's ugly from the outside but the food is delicious, so I forgive them."

Jessica grinned but Bethany struggled to keep her own smile. The differences were piling up, and that feeling of disappointment was welling again as she followed Jessica across the street and through the front door. A delicious blend of aromas assaulted her nose and she breathed them in.

"Yum."

Jessica cocked an eyebrow and smiled. "Indeed."

They were shown to their table and given menus.

"Can I get you some water, perhaps some bread and olives to start?" the waiter asked, his smile pleasant.

"Lovely," Bethany said, but Jessica frowned. "What?"

"Oh, sorry. Not a huge fan of olives."

"Okay. Well, you could order something else and I'll eat all the olives," Bethany said with a grin.

"I suppose…" Jessica looked up at the waiter. "Perhaps some hummus?"

"Of course."

They added a small carafe of the house white wine to their order, and he hurried off.

"So," Bethany said, looking up from the menu, "what do you recommend? It all sounds wonderful."

Jessica finally smiled, and Bethany breathed a subtle sigh of relief. "I can only speak for the vegetarian options, but they're all marvellous."

"Oh, I didn't realise you were veggie."

"Yes, my whole life. My parents were, and although they allowed me to choose my own path, I had no problem choosing to follow them. I detest the meat industry and all that it entails."

Bethany swallowed hard. "Well, I'll have a look at the vegetarian menu, then."

"You eat meat?" Jessica seemed surprised.

"Well, yes." Bethany shrugged. "Always have."

"Oh." Jessica dropped her gaze to her menu and Bethany had the distinct impression she had just fallen a significant level in Jessica's esteem.

She sighed and looked back to her own menu. Granted, the veggie options did all sound wonderful, so choosing something to eat wasn't that hard, but she couldn't help feeling she was compromising by doing so. Compromising as far as she had with Michelle? For one meal, perhaps not. But if she and Jessica were going to continue seeing each other, Bethany would have a real problem if she was going to be lectured on her choice of food all the time. Learning to deal with another person's needs was like walking a minefield. Why had she been so determined to do this dating thing again?

Trying not to groan out loud, she gripped her menu and made her choice. "Okay, I'm going to have the aubergine, and some mixed vegetables."

Jessica beamed. "Good choice. I'm having falafel with the trio of dips."

They placed their orders with the waiter, who had returned with the wine. When he had poured for them and left to attend to another table, Jessica raised her glass.

"To us, reconnecting after all this time." Her smile was warm, and her eyes shone in the low light of the restaurant. Once again, her beauty took Bethany's breath away, and all worries about the food and the compromising fell to the wayside.

"Hear, hear," Bethany replied, her voice a little raspy.

They chinked glasses and drank.

"So," Jessica said as she set her glass down, "what are your plans for the summer?"

Bethany grinned. "As little as possible."

Jessica tilted her head. "Meaning?"

"Well, the first week will be my usual lazy time at home alone, catching up on sleep. Then the second week is my annual holiday with my mum. We go to Cornwall to visit one of my aunts. She spoils us rotten, we eat too much, and then she sends us home with far too much clotted cream."

"Well, that sounds…lovely."

And there it was again, that hint of...rudeness in Jessica's response. As if she were sneering at Bethany's life choices.

"It is, actually," Bethany said, her tone strong and not sorry about it. "I'm very close to my mum, and it's always good for me to spend time with her."

"Oh, yes, I'm sure." Jessica's words were hurried, and her tone placating. "I didn't mean to suggest otherwise."

"Well, you know, it sounded like it." Bethany wasn't sure why she couldn't back down from this, but she had no regrets about plunging on. "That's the second or third time you've been a little snide about my choices in life, you know."

Jessica reeled back in her seat, her eyes wide. "I'm...I'm sorry, Bethany. But if I'm brutally honest, I think I always thought you would aim a little higher in life. I mean, I'm sure you find primary school fulfilling, but wouldn't you rather be working with more developed minds, shaping their thinking, showing them—"

Bethany snorted, which cut Jessica off mid-flow. "Wow, now you're really hitting low, Jessica. I *am* shaping their thinking, and I am helping, hugely, to develop those minds that come to you next. You should be thanking the likes of me, not belittling us."

Jessica stared at Bethany, who stared back.

"I've caused offence, and that wasn't my intention." Jessica's tone was meek, and her hands clasped together on the table in front of her. "Please accept my apologies, Bethany."

Breathing out slowly, Bethany nodded. "Accepted."

Their food was delivered, but Bethany's appetite had deserted her. She and Jessica were poles apart, and there was no glossing over that fact now. For all her outward beauty, there was something cold and snooty inside Jessica, and those were not characteristics Bethany wanted in a partner.

She picked at her food while they made desperate small talk, and it was easy to call for the bill as soon as Jessica had finished cleaning her plate.

"Was the food not good?" the waiter asked as he reached for Bethany's half-empty plate.

"It was lovely," she said sincerely, "I just wasn't as hungry as I thought. Sorry."

He smiled and cleared the table, returning with the bill moments later.

"Bethany," Jessica began, but she raised a hand.

"Jessica, it's been great to catch up with you again, but I think… Well, we're very different people, and I think we both know this isn't going to work."

Jessica slumped in her chair. "I know," she said, her voice not much more than a whisper.

Bethany pulled cash from her purse and laid it on the small dish which held the bill. Strangely, she felt good. Strong, and proud of herself for not pursuing something that in reality had not at all lived up to the fantasy she'd held in her mind for years.

Jessica added her money to the total, and they stood, in silence, and walked out of the restaurant.

"Goodbye, Bethany," Jessica said, not meeting her eyes. "I wish you well."

"And you," Bethany said, but she was already talking to Jessica's back as she marched up the road in the opposite direction from the Tube. Whichever way home she was taking, she wasn't taking it with Bethany, and that was just fine.

With a lightness in her step and a rueful grin, Bethany walked in the other direction towards the station.

At least she'd tried, and at least she would never wonder what if.

CHAPTER 10

"WELL, IT'S A SHAME THAT Jessica turned out to be such a snob," Alice said as she passed Bethany her cappuccino, "but at least you learned that pretty quickly."

"Yes, that's true." Bethany reached for the plastic knife and cut the sticky cinnamon bun in two. They were at the Starbucks near where Alice worked; Bethany had gone there straight from the school, and her mum was currently on a break so they could catch up. Bethany wasn't sure what she'd do if she didn't have her level-headed mum to talk things through with.

"And you have a lunch date with Sarah tomorrow, yes?"

Bethany nodded and passed her mum the other half of the bun. "Part of me thinks it's too soon after the disaster that was Tuesday night, but…"

Alice shrugged. "It's not like you have any lingering thoughts of Jessica to get in the way, other than knowing she's not the one for you. I say go for it."

Bethany let out a breath, and her mum tilted her head.

"What, love?"

"I didn't think it would be this hard. Which I know is completely unrealistic," she said as her mum made to interrupt. "But I was feeling so confident about getting out there again. I know, or at least I thought I knew, what I want, and I was all fired up to go get it." She shook her head. "But the reality of trying to find it is, well, sort of demoralising."

"Oh, come on," Alice huffed. "You've only been on two dates with two women. Things like this don't happen overnight, and you're smart enough to know that, aren't you?"

"Well, sorry, but you set such a high bar." Bethany smirked at her mother, then frowned when Alice looked confused. "You know, you and Dad, the amazing overnight romance, blah blah blah."

Alice's eyes popped wide and then she laughed out loud. "Oh, no! Is that what you've been thinking all these years?"

Now it was Bethany's turn to be confused. "You mean, it wasn't? But I thought—"

"Oh, Bethany." Alice was still chuckling. "Your dad was a prat the first time I met him. I dated several other men before I agreed to see him again. *Then* he was different, and *then* I fell in love with him." She shook her head. "Have you been thinking all this time that we had the perfect romance?"

Bethany nodded. "Well, of course! You two were amazing together, and you always told me there wasn't anyone else for you, and…"

"Yes, *after* we got together and he proved he was worth it. Before then, he annoyed the hell out of me, quite frankly." Alice leaned forward and patted her hand. "There's no such thing as perfect, love. If you're lucky, you find someone who ticks most of your boxes and then you work on the rest together. That's what your dad and I did, and yes, we were very, very happy. I want that for you too, but you are going to have to work for it, okay?"

Bethany didn't know what to say. All her life she'd idolised what her parents had. To learn now that it hadn't been that instant, just-like-in-the-movies love was a shock. At the same time, she found a measure of comfort in her mum's words. If it had worked for her parents in such spectacular fashion, maybe there was hope for her yet.

Throngs of people crowded the pavement that edged the south bank of the Thames, and Sarah wove her way between them as fast as she could. There was no way she wanted to be late. Bethany giving her a second chance was important, and she was determined to make it count.

She laughed at herself. This all still felt very strange. When Bethany had messaged her on Wednesday morning to confirm that their date was going ahead, she'd actually danced a few steps of delight across the office. Thankfully not in Roy's presence. So, Bethany had not fallen in love with the amazing Jessica from her past. Or, at least, not yet.

Her steps slowed. *Shit, I didn't think of that. What if Bethany hasn't quite written things off with that woman, and is just going out with me today as a sort of test, or for comparison purposes, or even worse, as some kind of pity date?*

She gazed out at the brown waters beside her as wavelets rippled across the river's surface in the wake of the multitude of craft out on its centre.

I'm getting all excited for this date and it might not be at all what I think it is.

A glance at her watch told her she had fifteen minutes to make it to the restaurant, and she was only five minutes away, so she continued at a slower pace, her thoughts racing.

Maybe I should just ask her, outright, as soon as we meet. Or would that put her off again, if I was that forthright up front?

Bloody hell, this dating business was a nightmare. No wonder she'd never really bothered with it before. She chuckled—she could almost hear Jonathan's eyes rolling at her for that thought.

You know what? Fuck it. I've got every right to ask what this is, and to make sure things are clear between us.

Mind made up, she squared her shoulders, upped her pace again, and strode off towards the restaurant. There was no sign of Bethany when she arrived, but she was still early. Their table was ready though, so she followed the waitress to it and sat down, laying her napkin on her lap and taking a few deep breaths to calm her nerves. She hated that she was nervous, a state of being she didn't often find herself in.

She reached for the menu and perused it while she waited. There were a number of items that had her mouth watering. Hell, even if Bethany didn't show, she'd stay and eat.

"Hi, Sarah."

Bethany's voice was low, but still Sarah nearly jumped out of her skin. How had she not seen or heard her approach?

"Bethany." She stood, and then wasn't sure why she had. It wasn't like she could give Bethany a kiss hello or anything, so she sat quickly, her cheeks burning. *Come on, Connolly, get a grip.* "Welcome," she said, pleased when her voice came out strong and clear. "Have a seat. You look lovely."

And she did. Bethany was wearing cropped jeans that finished just below her knees with a big turn-up, deck shoes, and a loose cotton shirt in a pale green colour that beautifully complemented the colour of her hair.

Bethany smiled and eased into the chair opposite. "Thank you. So do you." She tilted her head. "You looked surprised to see me just now."

Sarah responded without thinking. "Well, yes, a little. I did wonder if you would show."

Bethany winced and sat back in her chair. "Wow. Okay."

Sarah shrugged. "You had a date with this amazing woman from your past. Forgive me if I can't help wondering what's going on."

Puffing out a breath, Bethany relaxed her posture. "Fair enough." She looked away and sighed before turning back to Sarah. "The date with Jessica was…disappointing, to say the least. She's a shallow snob who thought I could have done so much better for myself."

"What?" Sarah's eyes went wide. "How rude."

Bethany chuckled. "Yes, it was. I couldn't get away quick enough," she said, and laughed.

"Oh, dear. I am sorry, but I'm also not, if you see what I mean." Sarah grinned.

"I do. And although it made me sad to discover she wasn't at all the person I thought she was, I'm glad I found that out quickly."

"I bet."

The waitress appeared, and they placed their orders, along with a glass of wine each and a bottle of water to share.

"So, in answer to your earlier question, what's going on is that I am now on a date with you. She is forgotten. This…" Bethany said, leaning forward slightly, "is us seeing if the good things we shared a couple of weeks ago can, I don't know, become something."

There was a mild sensation of panic in Sarah's stomach at Bethany's words, but it was quickly tamped down by the happier thought that this was, indeed, a full date with no hidden agendas.

Sarah raised her wineglass. "I can drink to that," she said, smiling, and hoping her nerves would settle soon so she could eat.

Bethany returned the smile and chinked her glass against Sarah's. Her eyes held Sarah's captive as they sipped.

"So how has school been the past couple of weeks?" she asked. "You finish soon, don't you?"

"Yes, three weeks to go. I'm definitely on the wind down, I think."

"I don't know how you do it." Sarah smiled. "I certainly wouldn't have the patience."

Bethany chuckled. "Yes, it really does need to be something you've always wanted to do, I think. Even then, the reality can be a little shocking."

"I'm sure it can! So it's really what you always wanted to do?"

"It really is. When I was a child I used to line my dolls up in class formation and read to them."

"That's brilliant, I can just imagine it! How cute." She finished with one of her flirtiest smiles. Bethany's answering blush triggered an indescribable feeling way down in Sarah's belly, and a deep smile spread across her face.

Their food arrived, and as they ate they chatted about the restaurant, Gabriel's Wharf in general, and the areas in which each of them lived.

"Oh, you're so lucky to be near water," Bethany exclaimed before tucking another forkful of risotto into her mouth.

"Yeah, I love it. It's best at night, or really early in the morning. I love watching the birds as they start their days, scurrying around for food, or nesting material if it's that time of year. And at night, it's just so calm out there, but you can still hear the water, because it's always on the move in some way or other. Sometimes I just sit out on my deck with a glass of wine and listen."

Bethany was gazing at her in unabashed appreciation and something warm curled its way outwards from Sarah's belly to the rest of her body.

"You are very beautiful," she murmured, allowing her gaze to roam just a little, down the line of Bethany's neck, laid bare by the open collar of her shirt, to the hint of cleavage that poked through from the wide V of the shirt.

"I... Thank you," Bethany croaked, blushing again. "You're gorgeous."

The words were a whisper, and it wasn't the first time anyone had said them to her, but this time they settled somewhere deep inside Sarah and lit a fire down low in her belly.

They stared at each other for a few moments, the air full of a sweet, delicious tension. Bethany broke it, in the end, swallowing hard and looking back down at the remains of her risotto before digging her fork in once again. Sarah returned to her pasta, her heart thudding.

"So, what else are you up to this weekend? And what's a regular weekend look like for you?"

Bethany smiled, and Sarah thought she detected a hint of relief that they were back to a safe subject.

"Well, every weekend usually involves baking something." She smiled shyly. "I'm a bit of a bakeaholic, if that's a word."

"It is now. You can claim it." Sarah sipped the last of her wine. "So what do you bake?"

Bethany shrugged. "All sorts. Biscuits, cakes, muffins, quiches. You name it, I bake it. Not bread so much, as I don't actually eat a lot of it, but I often make it in the winter to go with soups."

Sarah shook her head. "I'm impressed. I do cook, and I do okay with things like stir fries and curries. Oh, and barbecue. I am one mean barbecue chef, let me tell you." She smiled as Bethany laughed. "But baking is definitely not my thing."

"I just find it really relaxing and satisfying. I share most of what I make either with my family—my mum in particular—or with my fellow teachers. They're very appreciative."

"Well, yes, if you're bringing them free baked stuff every week, I'm sure they would be."

Bethany laughed.

They talked more about weekends, discovering a shared love of a few TV programmes, and for cheese.

"Oh, yeah, cheese is my kryptonite," Sarah said ruefully. "I really have to ration myself. I...I put on quite a bit of weight a few years back, so I'm careful with what I eat now that I've lost it all, and cheese goes straight to my hips if I'm not." It was sort of nervy, admitting that little bit of her past. She never talked about that kind of thing with her dates, usually because she was only concerned with the present, and getting women into her bed in the shortest amount of time possible. It was refreshing, actually conversing with someone first.

Sarah had to be honest and realistic with herself—getting Bethany into bed was still a goal, as always. But even as she had that thought, something squirmed inside her, leaving her feeling as if she'd not quite chewed that last bit of pasta properly before swallowing.

When they'd finished eating, they ordered coffees and took their time drinking them, both clearly unwilling to end the date.

"So do you like your job?" Bethany asked. "I mean, you told me you're a lawyer for a brokerage firm in the City, but you never actually said whether you like it."

Sarah surprised herself yet again when she waggled her hand in front of her in the universal gesture for "so-so". Her stock answer to that question was usually a robotic, "Yes, of course" before a swift change of subject.

"Explain," Bethany said. It was quirk of hers that was rapidly growing on Sarah, a tendency to use minimal words for key questions.

Sarah exhaled. "It's hard to explain, actually. It's not like I dread going in to work every morning. I'm always curious as to what the day will bring me."

She'd never told anyone any of this. Why couldn't she stop her mouth from talking? It was as if the part of her that held the normal routines and instructions had been replaced by a new handbook she'd had no time to read.

"I guess it's simply that I'm not practising the type of law I always dreamed of." She let out a half-laugh, half-snort. "When I was growing up, I always wanted to be a lawyer. I watched so many crime dramas on TV, and I wanted to be the one that got the guilty put away and saved the wrongly-accused from jail." She shrugged, and the sympathy in Bethany's eyes was nearly her undoing; the lump in her throat was so sudden she only just swallowed it down before anything embarrassing happened. "Corporate law for brokerage seems so very far from that dream."

"So why did you choose corporate law, rather than criminal?"

"My...father." She hesitated over the word; the background to that could definitely wait for another day. "He can be very persuasive. I think he genuinely worried about what criminal law might do to my mental health. He's a corporate lawyer too, so although he was thrilled I followed in his footsteps, he worked very hard to lure me away from the criminal side of things."

Bethany reached across the table and placed her hand on Sarah's. Her eyes were wide, as if she herself couldn't quite believe she was being so bold. It touched Sarah, and she smiled.

"I suppose I can understand why he did," Bethany said softly. "But it does seem a shame that you didn't get to live your dream."

Sarah didn't have a response to that, and was alarmed at the hint of moisture pricking at the corners of her eyes, so she quickly waved over the waiter and asked for the bill.

It was strange how rapidly the atmosphere had shifted when they'd started talking about Sarah's work. Bethany didn't want to push what seemed a sore subject, but at the same time she did want to know why Sarah had pretty much sprinted them out of the restaurant and back into the afternoon sunshine.

"Sarah, are you okay?"

She nodded but wouldn't meet Bethany's eye. "I'm fine. It's lovely out here, isn't it?"

There was a tightness to her voice that Bethany couldn't read, and without giving it a second's thought, she reached out and tugged on Sarah's arm.

Sarah turned to face her, but her expression was closed off, her gaze still not meeting Bethany's, and her arm twitched beneath Bethany's fingers.

"I've said it before, but I'll say it again," Sarah said, her voice husky. "You really are beautiful, Bethany."

In the next moment, their lips met and Sarah kissed her with a greediness that was momentarily thrilling, then rapidly became uncomfortable and unpleasant. Bethany pulled herself away, even as part of her wondered why the hell she was doing so.

"What the—?"

"Oh, come on, Bethany, you know you want to just as much as I do." Sarah's brown eyes, which had been warm and inviting, were now hard and flat.

"Not like that I don't," Bethany retorted, anger welling up. "For God's sake, Sarah, why did you do that? We've just been having a lovely time in there." She gestured to the restaurant behind them. "And now you pull a stunt like this? Just what is your problem? Every time we meet up I think it's going great and then you go and do something stupid to spoil it." Her voice had risen but she didn't care. This woman was so damn infuriating!

Sarah folded her arms across her chest, her stance defiant. "A kiss at the end of the date spoils it?" Her tone was snide, but there was something in her eyes, something like…panic.

"A kiss like that, yes," Bethany snapped, taking a step back.

Sarah stared at her for a few moments, then her eyes widened, her posture slumped, and she shook her head.

"God, I'm sorry. I… You know what, let's forget this. I can't do it. It's just not… Sorry," she said again, and before Bethany could respond she was gone, marching along the embankment by the river, her head bowed, her strides long.

CHAPTER 11

ALICE'S HANDS STILLED ON THEIR way to the teapot as Bethany finished her story and groaned in frustration.

"I honestly don't know what is wrong with that woman. Well," she huffed, "I don't actually have to worry anymore because that's clearly the last I've seen of her."

"Well, I should hope so. She doesn't sound like the sort of woman you need to be with at all," Alice said, finally pouring the tea and then walking over to the table with the two full mugs. She sat opposite Bethany and patted her hand. "I'm so sorry, love, that your dates aren't quite working out how you'd like."

Bethany flopped her head down onto her folded hands on the table. "I don't want to do this anymore. It's rubbish." Her voice was muffled but she knew her mum had heard her when she chuckled.

"You'll change your mind about that, I'm sure," Alice said. "You've got a whole summer ahead of you and therefore plenty of time to see who else is out there."

Bethany raised her head. "You choose."

"What?"

"You choose one for me. Set me up with a date. You must work with some nice women at the university."

Alice snorted. "Oh, Bethany, don't be ridiculous. I don't have the faintest idea of the sort of woman you'd like. Besides," she said, smiling wryly, "the only lesbian or bi women I know there are all in settled relationships already."

Bethany groaned and flopped her head back down again. "Then I'm doomed."

"Bethany Keane, get a hold of yourself," Alice said, her voice strident.

Looking up, Bethany smiled despite herself. Her mum had her "I'm going to tell you something important and you'd better listen to me" face on.

"You were raised to be a woman who knows her own mind. To not be afraid to be who you are, and to follow your heart. To speak out whenever you are not happy, and to not settle for anything less than what truly makes you happy. Yes?"

"Yes, Mum," Bethany mumbled. When her mum started this speech, there was no point in arguing with her. Besides, she was, of course, right.

"So, you are going to pick yourself up, dust yourself off, and get right back on that horse again, yes?"

"Yes, Mum."

"Good. Now," Alice said, leaning forward, her gaze keen. "What about online dating?"

"You did *what*?" Jonathan's voice was tight, and when he put his hands on his hips, Sarah knew she was in for a rough ride.

"I just…panicked," she mumbled.

"Panicked?"

"Things were getting, you know, emotional and…"

"And so you thought being overly physical would allow you to hide from your emotions, yes?"

Sarah stared at him. Damn, he was good.

Jonathan marched across the kitchen to a corked bottle of red wine on the counter, yanked out the cork and brought the bottle back to the table. He went back for two glasses from the cabinet on the other wall, then sat down opposite her at the kitchen table and poured them each a glass of the ruby liquid.

"Thank you," Sarah whispered.

"Whatever," he muttered, before taking a healthy mouthful.

"Sarah, dear, how lovely to see you." Evelyn appeared in the doorway, having presumably just awoken from her afternoon nap. "It is Saturday, don't you have better places to be than here?"

"She was," Jonathan said acidly, "but she blew it."

Evelyn walked slowly over to the table and pulled out the chair next to Sarah's.

Jonathan stood. "Tea, Evelyn?"

"Yes, please. Some Darjeeling, I think."

Jonathan nodded and went to the counter to carry out his task. Sarah watched him, not daring to meet her aunt's eyes. Evelyn's surprisingly strong fingers on her forearm forced her to turn and face the older woman.

"Sarah?"

Sighing, Sarah slumped back in her chair. "I had a second date with Bethany."

"The same woman from a couple of weeks ago? The one who stormed out on you?"

Chuckling ruefully, Sarah nodded.

"I did not realise you were such a glutton for punishment," Evelyn said, her frown deep.

Blinking rapidly as thoughts of an entirely different nature invaded her brain at Evelyn's choice of words, Sarah cleared her throat before speaking.

"Well, she's lovely. And I like her very much. I just..."

"Keep blowing it," Jonathan finished for her from across the room.

"Ha bloody ha," Sarah mumbled.

"Well, that's not the end of the world, is it? There are, as that delightful old saying goes, plenty more fish in the sea, dear." Evelyn accepted the tea Jonathan handed to her and sat back with a contented look on her face.

Jonathan scowled. "Yes, but Sarah's had most of them by now."

"Hey!" Sarah sat upright, indignant. "I'm not that bad!"

Sighing, Jonathan sat down opposite her. "No, you're not. But I do wish you'd try something a little different. I was so hopeful when you asked Bethany out again."

So was I. Why can't I just do this, actually date someone? Why can't I just be...normal?

"I was too," she whispered, and smiled when Jonathan's eyebrows shot up.

"Well, that's some admission," he said, nodding slowly.

A noisy, less-than-ladylike slurp of tea came from Sarah's left and she looked round at her aunt, who was frowning as she put her cup back down.

"Something to say, aunty dear?"

Evelyn tutted. "I simply do not understand why you are fighting your nature, Sarah. You have always been on the move, exploring all that life has to offer, and you have enjoyed it immensely. Trying to do something different is making you unhappy, so..." She gave an elegant shrug of her shoulders.

"But she hasn't explored *everything* that life has to offer," Jonathan said, his tone far gentler than it had been so far. He stared at Sarah. "You haven't explored what being in love is like, and all the wonder that can bring to a person."

Sarah swallowed hard. *Love?* She loved Evelyn, and Jonathan, and, in her own way, her parents. But it was true, she'd never been *in love* with someone. What would that even feel like? Was she capable of it? Did she want it?

"Love is overrated," Evelyn said, to a loud tut from Jonathan.

"Love is the most wonderful feeling in the world," he countered, with passion.

"Stop forcing her into something she does not want," the older woman said. "Can't you see how much it is unsettling her?"

"Evelyn, I'm not forcing her into anything. I am simply giving her an alternative view on the options in front of her."

Evelyn grumbled something indecipherable and reached for her tea.

"Sarah, apart from the rather unfortunate ending to the date, how do you feel about what happened with Bethany? And would you like to see her again?"

Sarah held his intense gaze. "I loved it," she whispered. "I just... I really like her, and I really, *really* want her. But I also know who I am. That if I'd taken her home with me tonight, I probably wouldn't have called her ever again. And I don't want to do that to her. And I think that's why I made such a mess of things. I was trying so hard not to hurt her one way, I hurt her in another way. I tell you, this dating thing is a bloody minefield." She punctuated her words with another swig of wine.

"And did you get the impression she wanted to see you again?"

Sarah nodded. "Oh, yeah. I mean, I'm not bragging, but yeah. Until I screwed it up, of course."

"Oh, Sarah," Jonathan said, shaking his head. "What are we going to do with you?"

"We are going to leave her alone," Evelyn chimed in. "Sarah does not need us pushing her into something she is not ready for."

"But I think she *is* ready for this. I think she always has been, and your meddling hasn't helped her in that."

"Meddling?" Evelyn's voice went up an octave. "I have looked after Sarah a lot longer than you have, young man, and I know more about her life and her needs, and I will continue to look out for her as long as I still have breath in my lungs."

Jonathan and Evelyn glared at each other across the table.

"Hey, time out, you two." Sarah reached out to both of them. "Come on, seriously, this is not worth you two falling out over." They both relaxed a little, and she squeezed their arms. "I know you both care about me, in your own ways. And I've always appreciated the advice you give me, even if I haven't always agreed with it."

She turned to Evelyn. "I know you worry about my wellbeing, about my mental health, after all that you saw me do to myself back then. But really, Evelyn, I do think I'm in a different place now. There is something about Bethany that pulls me to her. Something that means I do want to see what can happen with this, even though it scares the sh—the poo out of me."

Evelyn sighed, and her eyes glistened. "I know, Sarah dear. I just cannot help but worry."

Sarah's throat tightened. "I know. But honestly, if you met her, you'd see what I'm talking about."

"Well," Evelyn said, sniffing and wiping at her eyes. "Maybe that could happen one day."

Sarah smiled, and swallowed hard. "Yes, maybe it could."

She gave Evelyn's arm another squeeze, then looked at Jonathan.

"And you," she said, "need to stop berating me when I get this dating thing wrong. I have no idea what I'm doing, but at least I'm trying, okay?"

Jonathan looked abashed. "You're right, darling. I'm sorry."

He stood up and walked round the table to give her a long hug.

"I am so proud of you for trying," he whispered before pulling back. "And I'm sorry I'm giving you such a hard time. I just don't want you to blow this."

"I know. And I get that. But you've got to help me out here. What do I do next?"

To her surprise, it was her aunt who spoke. "You need to call her, dear, and apologise." Evelyn smiled. "And ask her out again. Perhaps send some flowers. Or maybe chocolates."

"Oooh, I like those ideas," Jonathan said, grinning. "You should listen to your aunt. She's wise beyond her years."

He looked across the table at Evelyn and winked.

Evelyn just rolled her eyes and sipped her tea.

Starbucks was full, as usual for a lunchtime, but Sarah actually didn't mind. Her thoughts were still spinning from the weekend's events, and her aunt's advice to simply call Bethany up. Only it wasn't that simple, not for someone who had no experience with this whole let's-have-more-than-one-date shebang. One minute she knew Evelyn was right, the next she was cursing her for suddenly taking Jonathan's side. She'd managed a short text message of apology to Bethany on Sunday, but that hadn't garnered any response, and now she was facing the excruciating dilemma of whether to follow up with a call or just give up on the whole thing entirely.

Someone tapped her on the shoulder.

"Your turn," a male voice said.

Snapping out of her reverie, she noticed the barista waiting to take her order and smiled at her before turning back to thank the man who'd brought her back to the present. She grinned when she saw it was Scott Fisher.

"Sorry, I was miles away."

"Oh, hey, Sarah!" He smiled. "No worries."

She placed her order, and Scott moved to the order point next to her, where he was greeted by the cute male barista she'd seen working here many times before.

"Hi, what can I get you?" the man asked with a flirty smile and a flick of his long fringe.

"Skinny latte, please."

"If you don't mind me saying, that's a lovely suit." The barista was beaming, and Sarah nearly laughed out loud at the way he leaned forward, thrusting his chest into Scott's space.

"Oh, er, thanks. Had it for years." Scott seemed taken aback by the attention, and Sarah was astonished. Surely he realised how gorgeous he was, and how appealing he would therefore be to the rest of the gay male population?

"Well, it totally suits you." The barista giggled at his dreadful joke and Sarah cringed with embarrassment on his behalf.

When Scott didn't respond, the barista stopped laughing and took his cash. However, as Scott made to move away from the counter, the barista held up one finger, glanced quickly around, then reached for a napkin and pen and scribbled something before sliding the napkin across the counter towards him.

Scott visibly sighed, reached for the napkin, and scrunched it into his pocket. He moved off, Sarah trailing behind him, her curiosity peaked.

"I imagine that happens a lot to you, yes?" she said in an undertone as they made their way to the end of the counter.

Scott tutted. "Unfortunately, yes."

Suddenly thinking her gaydar must be malfunctioning, she cleared her throat and said, "Sorry, I must confess, I thought you were gay too."

Scott turned to stare at her, then laughed. "Oh, I am."

"But then…"

"Not my scene," he said, his tone curt. "I'm holding out for Mr Right."

Jesus, not another one! Why did everyone except her think that being in love was the be all and end all? Before she could think to censor herself, the words spilled out. "Good God, what is it with you gay men and your big thing about happy bloody ever after?"

His eyes narrowed. "What, you think you lesbians have monopolised the market on U-hauls?" He turned away from her to grab his coffee. When he turned back, his face was set in a frown. "And trust me, I wish I could find another gay man who wanted the whole commitment thing, but they seem to be a rare breed these days." He stared at her a moment. "You have no idea how easy you have it."

With that, he turned away and left. Sarah, her conscience finally kicking in and giving her a boot up the backside, grabbed her own drink and hurried after him.

"Scott! Scott, wait. Please!"

He didn't slow. She could just leave it; after all, she barely knew him. But she knew she'd been unfair and it didn't sit right with her. So, careful to avoid spilling her drink, she increased her speed until she caught up with him.

"Scott, I'm so sorry. I...I've got some stuff going on and I just spoke without thinking. Please accept my apologies. I didn't mean to paint you as any kind of stereotype."

He slowed and turned to glance at her. Whatever he saw on her face relaxed his frown, and he nodded.

"Apology accepted."

They walked on in silence for a few moments.

"Need someone to talk to?" he asked, eventually. "It's not that homophobic prick you work with, is it? Because I will happily go to HR with you if that's—"

"No, no, it's not him. Although good to know you'd back me up if it came to it."

He grinned, and she smiled.

"I thought dickheads like him had died out years ago," he said, shaking his head.

"He's old school, I'm afraid. A dying breed, sure, but they're not quite extinct yet."

"Ain't *that* the truth," he said, feigning an American accent.

She laughed, then sobered. "So, you're single?"

He nodded, then took a sip of his drink before shrugging his shoulders. "It's all about the hook-ups out there right now. And that's never what I've wanted. Even less now." He smiled ruefully. "I'm not getting any younger, you know."

She nudged his shoulder. "You don't look a day over thirty."

"Oh, I like you!" He nudged her back, then leaned down to whisper, "Thirty-eight next month."

"You wear it well," she said, appraising him and grinning as he fanned himself.

"What about your love life?" he asked, and she nearly choked on her drink.

"Me? Um, well, it's…it's complicated."

He rolled his eyes. "Isn't it always with you dykes?"

Sarah laughed out loud.

When the email reminder arrived on Wednesday evening, Bethany sighed. How could she have forgotten? Well, actually, that had been easy, what with everything she'd had on her mind.

Bondage for Beginners Evening Workshop
Thursday 5th July 6.30pm

She'd signed up weeks ago, long before the dating fiasco started, thinking the class would be a safe environment for her to explore some of the things that had dominated—she snorted at her own pun—her fantasies over the last year or so. The class was part of a series run by the sex shop where she'd bought her vibrator, and they had a good reputation for running informative and relaxing classes where boundaries were greatly respected.

Maybe she should just cancel. She'd lose her fee this close to the time, but…

She sat up on the sofa. No. Her mum was right—she was raised to be strong, to know her own mind, and to follow her own path. Going to this class would be a big step forward in discovering her true sexual self, so no, she wasn't going to back out of it now.

After closing down the email app on her phone, she couldn't stop herself from scrolling back to the message app, and the text that Sarah had sent to her on Sunday morning:

> *Bethany, I am so sorry for my behaviour at the end of our date yesterday. It was unacceptable, and it certainly did spoil what had been a lovely afternoon up to that point. I would like to explain to you what happened, and see if we can start again. Can we meet? Call me, please?*

ONE WAY OR ANOTHER

The message had caused Bethany great confusion. She'd left the wharf on Saturday adamant that Sarah was gone from her life—someone so unpredictable was not who Bethany envisaged trying to build a relationship with. Even if that someone was intelligent, witty, full of life, and stunning to look at. Then she'd woken to that message on Sunday and was instantly conflicted again. Sarah sounded so sincere, and her offer to explain was a pleasant surprise. But then, this was the Jekyll-and-Hyde behaviour she'd already displayed twice since they'd met, and it gave Bethany pause for thought.

She hadn't replied, or called, and a part of her felt guilty about that. Sarah hadn't messaged again, and while Bethany was grateful that Sarah wasn't pushing, she couldn't help worrying she'd hurt her a little by ignoring the attempt to make things right between them.

Groaning, she stood up and walked to the kitchen. She needed to put thoughts of Sarah out of her mind and focus on work tomorrow, and that bondage class. She chuckled. Well, there was a sentence she'd never have imagined putting together in her brain.

Thankfully her pupils were angelic on Thursday, and her work day flew by in a pleasant rush, without any drama. She hurried home to change; she had no idea what was appropriate to wear, but as the shop had recommended something casual and comfortable, she'd chosen her soft, skinny blue jeans and a loose cotton shirt, the brown sister of the green one she'd worn on the date with Sarah.

She tutted as she did up the buttons. *Not supposed to be thinking about her, remember?*

Finally ready, she grabbed her handbag and headed out to the Tube. There was a light summer rain falling so she hurried along underneath her umbrella, dodging small puddles and other pedestrians.

As she neared the shop, her heart rate sped up. She was excited and nervous all at the same time, and now wishing she had a friend who could have accompanied her. Of course, that thought just made her laugh—none of her friends, most of whom were straight, were close enough that she'd have felt comfortable asking them.

The shop was busy, and it sent her nerves rocketing. She shuffled in between two couples who were each discussing the merits—or not—of the glass dildos on a special display in the centre of the shop, and approached the counter. The woman behind it, a different one from when she'd been there before, smiled broadly at her.

"Hi, can I help?"

Bethany nodded and leaned in. "Yes," she said quietly, "I'm here for the class."

"Perfect," the woman said. "You're a little early, so please just feel free to browse around the store. We've already announced that casual shoppers only have five minutes left before we close for the class, so it won't be long. Okay?"

Nodding again, and smiling as best she could, Bethany backed away from the counter and stepped on someone's foot.

"Ouch!" a quiet voice said.

"Sorry," Bethany said, whirling around, "I was—"

It was Sarah.

Bethany didn't know who was the more shocked of the two of them. They stared wide-eyed at each other for a few moments before Sarah's mouth curled into a small but sad smile.

"Hi, Bethany."

"Hi." Bethany swallowed. "I'm, um, sorry about your foot."

Sarah shrugged. "No worries. I'll live."

She stared at Bethany, and her gaze held so much it took Bethany's breath away. There was sorrow there, and regret, and once again that obvious appreciation that sent shivers tumbling down Bethany's spine. Argh, why did this woman keep doing this to her?

"I'm sorry I didn't call," she said quietly.

Sarah shook her head. "It's okay."

She looked away as the shop assistant announced that the store was closing to all but those registered for the class. Bethany blushed. *Oh God, now Sarah's going to know why I'm here.*

"Hi, Sarah," the assistant said as she walked past them to usher the last stragglers out of the shop.

"Hey," Sarah replied, her head still turned away from Bethany.

Why isn't she moving? She should be leaving, right?

Oh, God. She's not leaving.

She's here for the class too.

Bethany wanted to groan out loud but managed to suppress it. This was so ridiculously unfair. Sarah was the last person on Earth Bethany wanted in the room when she learned about tying up a lover. Especially when some of her fantasies recently had featured Sarah being tied up by her, and it was obvious from Sarah's personality that there was no way she was here to learn the ropes, so to speak, as a submissive.

So bloody unfair.

Sarah turned back around and seemed startled to see Bethany still standing there. Eyes wide, she said, "Are you…? The…the class?"

Struck dumb, Bethany merely nodded.

"Oh." Sarah's eyes narrowed then, and she ran a hand through her hair. "Well, um, this isn't awkward at all, is it?"

Bethany barked out a laugh and Sarah grinned, shaking her head.

"Jesus," Sarah whispered. She cleared her throat. "You know what, I think I'll go." She took a couple of steps back. "Enjoy the class."

What?

"Sarah, wait," Bethany blurted. "You don't have to—"

"It's okay, Bethany. I'll catch the next one." Sarah smiled, and it was full of such honesty and openness that Bethany's stomach did a flip. "I'll… Goodbye, Bethany."

Bethany watched her walk over to the assistant, say a few words, then walk out of the shop. Leaving was extraordinarily generous, and thoughtful, and…lovely of Sarah. Sure, there may have been an element of self-preservation in the act, but Bethany couldn't help feeling that it was mostly all about making things easier for her.

Once again, Sarah had managed to confuse the hell out of her, and it was just as infuriating as before.

"Okay everyone, I think we're ready to start," the shop assistant called.

Bethany sighed and rolled her eyes. Well, if there was one good thing that came out of seeing Sarah tonight, it was that Bethany was no longer nervous about the class. And that was because the class was now the last thing on her mind; Sarah, once again, occupied all the available space therein.

CHAPTER 12

THERE WAS A SPRING IN Bethany's step all the way home, and it wasn't just from all that she had learned about bondage ties, restraints, and cuffs. Sarah sacrificing the class for her had stayed with her throughout the event, as had the warm feelings it had engendered for the dark-haired woman who caused her such a maelstrom of confusion and attraction.

When she walked through her front door, the idea that had been forming in her brain on the Tube took shape and grabbed hold of her. She threw her handbag on the sofa after pulling out her mobile phone from its depths and, before she could out-think herself, rang Sarah's number.

Sarah picked up on the third ring, and her surprise was evident in her greeting. "Bethany?"

"Hi, Sarah." Bethany walked a circle around her coffee table, trying to keep her breathing even. "Is this an okay time to call?"

"Absolutely. Yes. Of course." Her words were rushed, and it made Bethany smile.

"I just... I wanted to say thank you, for giving up the class tonight. I didn't say it in the shop, which was very rude of me, but you shocked me so much by doing that, it—"

"Hey, it's okay. No thanks necessary. It was just the right thing to do." Sarah's tone was earnest.

"It was very thoughtful and generous, and I really appreciate it."

"Well, you're welcome." Sarah paused, then said, "So, good class?"

Blushing even though Sarah couldn't see her, and cursing herself for still having this reaction to her own sexual explorations, Bethany said, "It was. Yes."

"Good."

She didn't push, and Bethany shook her head again at how *nice* this version of Sarah was.

"So, um, I was wondering," Bethany said, her voice a little croaky. "In your message on Sunday you said you, um, wanted to explain about how our date ended, and, well, I was wondering if you would like to meet up to talk." She sighed. "I'll be honest, Sarah, you infuriate me. One minute you're super nice and lovely to spend time with, the next you're..."

"Psycho crazy woman?" Sarah offered.

"Well, yes. Sort of."

Sarah chuckled, then sighed. "Bethany, I am so sorry. And yes, there is an explanation and it does not, I hasten to point out, involve anything like an actual disorder or drugs or anything, okay?"

"Okay."

"So," Sarah said on a long breath, "I have an idea. Are you free on Saturday?"

"I am. Although not too early, please."

Sarah's laugh was warm and gentle. "No worries about that. I was wondering about a picnic somewhere. What do you think? Too lame?" Sarah sounded unsure, and nervous. Bethany practically melted.

"I think a picnic sounds amazing," she said quietly.

"Brilliant." Sarah sounded relieved now. "I know it's a little out of your way, but can I suggest the Olympic Park in Stratford? There's some beautiful spots along the river."

"Oh, I would love that!" Bethany grinned. "I've never been and have always meant to."

"Then that's what we'll do. I'll text you where to meet."

"Great, thank you. What shall we do for food? Each bring something? I'll bake something, if you like."

"Oh, that would be amazing. Yes, please!" Sarah seemed genuinely delighted at the idea, not just being polite, and that thought sent a warm wave spreading through Bethany's body. "And I'll grab us some other things from M&S on my way home tomorrow. How does that sound?"

"That sounds wonderful," Bethany said, before she could censor herself.

Sarah sighed. "It really does," she said quietly. "Bethany, thank you for agreeing to meet. I'm...I'm really looking forward to it."

The intensity of her voice sent a thrill coursing through Bethany's body.

Friday evening saw Sarah spending a ridiculous amount of time perusing—and agonising over—the variety of picnic-suitable food on sale in the M&S Food at Liverpool Street station. She had forgotten to ask Bethany if she had any food preferences or allergies, and after spending five minutes trying to second-guess, gave in and sent her a text.

I'm buying food for tomorrow - anything I should avoid?!

Bethany's response came only a few moments later, complete with smiley face emoji.

Anything is good. Oh, except coriander - yuk!

Sarah chuckled and texted a "thanks" in response with a laughing face emoji.

She was feeling relaxed, and light-hearted, and hopeful, all of which were combining to keep a grin permanently locked on her face. She was so glad the picnic idea had been a hit—it was something she'd begrudgingly sought Jonathan's advice over. To his credit, he'd kept his usual sarcasm in check.

"A picnic?" he'd said, when she'd called him right after getting off the phone with Bethany. "What made you think of that?"

"Well, I just thought it was kind of…safer, for her. No pressure, you know? And you know I like being outdoors, so I took a gamble on her feeling the same way."

"And it worked beautifully. That is extremely thoughtful of you, Sarah. Well done."

"Shit, I'm just making it up as I go along," Sarah said, which earned her a loud tut.

"I do wish you wouldn't keep downplaying your own sensitivity," he said, sounding irritated. "This cold-hearted bitch impression you like to present to the world is getting a tad tiresome."

"Consider me admonished," she retorted.

"You know I'm right. Stop fighting it," he said, before moving on to a discussion about what sort of foods she should take for the picnic.

Of course, all advice on that score deserted her the minute she was faced with the amount of food available, and so here she was, floundering around the refrigerated section trying not to be bamboozled by what was on offer.

Twenty minutes later she was at the cash desk, piling what was probably way too much food onto the counter. She'd have to re-evaluate in the morning; she'd never be able to carry it all.

After lugging everything home and storing it appropriately, she decided on a workout to ease her nerves. The unpleasant realisation that she *was* nervous had hit her on the way home on the train. Her self-confidence had always been strong, especially since university, where she'd excelled at both the studying and partying aspects. She had progressed rapidly in her career on the back of that confidence, impressing everywhere she went. Who would have thought that a somewhat geeky primary school teacher would be the one to turn her into a bag of nerves the night before a simple picnic date?

Maybe it was because Bethany was so different from all the other women Sarah had taken to her bed. Maybe it was because, for once, taking Bethany to bed was not Sarah's primary objective. That time in the wine bar—which seemed ages ago now, even though it was a mere three weeks—it had been, but now... Just the thought of seeing Bethany again made Sarah smile, no matter what they ended up doing.

She headed to the workout room, stripping off her suit as she went, leaving behind a trail of clothes that she'd pick up later. As she changed into her Lycra and trainers, she shook her head in wonder at what was happening to her.

It was weird.

Like, *really* weird.

But good.

Bethany groaned as the unmistakeable smell of burned pastry assaulted her nostrils when she returned to the kitchen. She hauled the tin containing the quiche out of the oven and stared forlornly at it.

Ruined.

Somehow she'd forgotten to set the timer, which was unheard of for her. Then she'd wandered off to the bedroom to try to decide what to wear for the picnic, and now she had a burned quiche in her hands.

She glanced at her watch; just enough time. Chopping and beating furiously, mentally berating herself the entire time, she whipped up another quiche and put it in the oven. She resolutely set two timers—one in the kitchen and one on her phone in the bedroom—and returned to her outfit dilemma.

The weather forecast was good—twenty-six degrees, sunny all day, and only a light breeze. She'd need some sunscreen, for sure. Shorts was probably also the way to go—if she felt brave enough to show her legs—or maybe those light blue cropped trousers she'd bought last year... When she'd finally made a decision, she grabbed a quick shower.

Once the new, near-perfect quiche had been retrieved from the oven and placed on a cooling rack, she sat on the sofa and tried to relax. The thought of seeing Sarah again was both exhilarating and nerve-wracking.

While Bethany wasn't a virgin, she may as well have been for all the experience she'd had—or not—in the last seven years. Sex with her one and only girlfriend, Michelle, in college had been...satisfactory. Not earth-shattering, as they'd both been virgins and had stumbled their way through the basics a few times before they finally got the hang of the essentials. But their relationship, if you could call it that, had been relatively short-lived—three months after it started it petered out. Michelle didn't enjoy playing second fiddle to Bethany's studies, and Bethany wasn't about to jeopardise her dream of becoming a teacher for endless sex-filled nights with Michelle.

Since then, Bethany had relied on fantasies about Jessica, or the other crushes she'd had over the years, and erotic books, and the internet, along with her right hand, to meet any sexual urges she'd had. There hadn't been that many, and for some time she'd wondered if she was actually asexual. But some research on some excellent websites, and an honest and in-depth self-assessment had left that idea behind. She definitely did want a relationship with someone that included sex, but until now, hadn't figured out how to fit that and her career together. Meeting Sarah had opened that idea up—exploded it, actually—as Sarah was the kind of sexy woman Bethany had only ever dreamed about meeting.

And if they became a something, they'd probably end up having sex. Although, if she was honest with herself, she did have some doubts about how compatible they might be in bed. She knew exactly what she was looking for, and somehow the confident, experienced Sarah didn't fit the image of the submissive lover Bethany desired. But taming someone as bold as Sarah would be even more exciting, wouldn't it? Getting someone that confident to submit to her will and desires, to be able to pin her down, tie her up, take her every which way she wanted—

Bethany sat upright on the sofa, her skin flushing, and wondrous sensations pinpricking between her legs. That line of thought needed to be headed off right now; she couldn't go into her date with Sarah with her underwear already wet.

A glance at the clock on the small mantel told her she needed to leave in ten minutes anyway, so she distracted herself with teeth cleaning, hair brushing—again—and finding a suitable container and strong bag to carry the quiche in, along with the scones and jam she'd put together much earlier that morning.

Sarah's directions were crystal clear, and Bethany's heart thumped beneath her ribs as she spotted her waiting at their allotted meeting place. As Bethany's steps took her to within arm's reach of Sarah, she hesitated, wondering if they should hug, or kiss on the cheek, or—

Sarah smiled warmly and leaned forward to lightly kiss Bethany on the cheek, and Bethany closed her eyes against the tumult of sensation that simple touch bestowed.

Good grief, get a hold of yourself.

"You look great," Bethany said, letting her gaze take in the wondrous sight of Sarah in casual clothes—cropped jeans hugged her legs from her hips to just below her knees, small tears and holes in the denim revealing tantalising glimpses of tanned flesh beneath. Her sleeveless top was white, emphasising her tanned arms, and it was scooped low in the neck, which drew Bethany's gaze unerringly to the dip of cleavage it revealed.

Bethany's mouth went dry.

"Thanks," Sarah murmured. "So do you."

Bethany forced her gaze away from Sarah's chest to find Sarah looking at her, her eyes slightly glazed, her tongue moistening her lips. They stared at each other for a moment before Sarah seemed to snap out of her daze, then bent to pick up the large basket at her feet, which she lifted effortlessly.

"Shall we?" She gestured behind her.

Bethany nodded and stepped alongside her. "Do you need me to carry anything?"

Sarah turned to smile at her. "No, I'm good." She walked on a few paces. "So, if you haven't been here before, would you like the tour now or later?"

Bethany looked at the large basket in Sarah's arms, and down at the large bag she herself carried. "How about later? When we have less to carry?"

Sarah's smile lit up her face. "Yes, that sounds like a good idea. Thank you."

They walked in comfortable silence, past Stratford International station, catching glimpses of the stadium in the distance, then through the residential area of the park before crossing a road that led to a picnic area with public barbecue stations.

"Here?" Bethany asked, looking around as they wandered through.

"No, there's much better spots along the river itself, if you don't mind walking a little further?"

Bethany smiled. "The river sounds lovely."

They followed a winding pathway past some small ponds surrounded by reeds and trees. "I had no idea this was here," Bethany said, looking round in wonder.

"I know, it's marvellous what they did here. I come here a lot to just sit and watch the river."

After a few more minutes, Sarah led them across a bridge over the River Lea, and up a slight grassy incline. "Here, if that's okay? It's comfortable to sit on, and we can look over the water."

"It's perfect," Bethany said, gazing at the gorgeous view. On the path they'd just left, walkers and joggers passed by, families and couples strolling and chatting. But up here on the grass, there were only two other couples sharing the space, and she and Sarah spread their blankets out to make a very spacious and comfortable picnic area. They opened all of the food, laying it out smorgasbord style, and Bethany laughed at just how much Sarah had bought.

"Were you hungry when you shopped?" she asked, chuckling.

Sarah blushed. "I was, yes. And I had no idea what you liked, and didn't want you to have too little to eat, so…"

She looked very embarrassed, way more than the situation warranted, so Bethany decided to be bold and reached out to take Sarah's hand. Sarah stared at her, wide-eyed, then down at their joined hands.

"Thank you," Bethany said softly. "That's very sweet of you."

"You're welcome."

They loaded up their plates—Sarah had brought two fancy plastic picnic plates and full cutlery for both of them—and sat back to munch. They ate in silence for a while, exchanging glances and small smiles, and murmurs of appreciation for the flavours on their plates.

"I didn't realise how hungry I was until I saw this all laid out," Bethany managed to say around a mouthful of couscous salad.

Sarah chuckled. "Me neither. This quiche is incredible! You can seriously cook, Bethany."

She flushed under the praise. "Aw, thanks. I'm so glad you like it."

Sarah took another mouthful and hummed, which made Bethany laugh, then pushed her plate away. "Okay, enough. For now. I'm sure I'll want seconds later." She stopped and stared at Bethany. "Sorry, perhaps that was a little presumptuous. I mean, I'm hoping we can spend all afternoon together but if—"

"I'm sure we will," Bethany interrupted gently. "But that might depend on what you have to say for yourself." She smiled after she spoke, but Sarah still looked uncomfortable. "Sorry, I meant that to be cheeky, not as if I was delivering some kind of ultimatum."

"Actually, I think you have every right to deliver one. On both our dates I've been an absolute asshole. Again, I am so grateful that you've given me this chance."

"So," Bethany said, placing her own plate to one side and leaning back on her elbows, bracing herself both physically and mentally for what was to come. "Are you ready to talk to me?"

Sarah swallowed and nodded. She swivelled so she was fully facing Bethany, her back to the river. She blinked a couple of times, then inhaled deeply.

"Okay." She shook her head. "God, I am completely rubbish at this. Sorry." After a couple more breaths, she tried again. "So, the thing is, up until now, I've never really been in a relationship."

What? How was that possible?

Bethany's confusion must have been clear on her face, since Sarah chuckled. "I said relationship. Trust me, I've been involved with many women." She sighed. "I'm trying something new with you—getting to know you, seeing what we might be. It's not my normal method of operation, and, as you have unfortunately seen, some of my habits from my former, um, lifestyle, have taken over. Especially on Saturday, after I'd told you all that stuff about my career and my father. I don't normally open up like that."

"It scared you." The realisation was so clear it almost made Bethany smile as so many things slotted into place.

"Exactly." Sarah looked away. "Somehow there is something different about me when I'm with you. And I like it, but it scares me." She shrugged, her eyes meeting Bethany's again. "I have no idea if I can do this, but I really want to try. I really like you, Bethany." A blush coloured her cheeks, but she held Bethany's gaze. "And I know I need to take things slow with you. That, you know, any physical intimacy needs to come a lot later."

Bethany startled. "What makes you say that?"

"Um, well." Sarah scratched absently at the back of her neck. "I guess I thought from our first meeting at the sex shop, and our first date, that you were a little...shy? Inexperienced, perhaps? Sorry, maybe that's not fair to say."

Bethany shrugged. "No, it's true. I am both of those things." She squared her shoulders slightly. "But that doesn't mean I don't know what I want," she said firmly.

Sarah's eyes went wide, and she cleared her throat again before saying, "You do? I mean, I suppose you must do. You were at that class on Thursday, after all."

"Um, well. Yes." Bethany sat up then. "Thank you for explaining. It does make a lot of sense now." She smiled. "I suppose all I can say is, let's see how we go, yes? And that it's okay to tell me if something makes you nervous, preferably before you do something Neanderthal again."

Sarah laughed, her shoulders shaking. "Okay, that's fair."

They spent another two hours on the blankets, eating and talking, sipping slowly at the chilled wine Sarah had packed in its own thermal sleeve inside the basket. Bethany feasted slowly, both on the wonderful spread they'd put together, and on the sight of Sarah lounging across the blanket in front of her. It was relaxed, and fun, and exactly what Bethany wanted. They talked about their favourite films, books, and food, and Bethany talked about her family, but Sarah was less than forthcoming on that aspect of her life, and Bethany didn't want to push, especially after what Sarah had said about opening up. There'd be time for that. Hopefully.

"God, take this quiche away from me," Sarah groaned as she cut herself yet another sliver.

Bethany chuckled. "I'm glad you like it so much."

"It's amazing," Sarah said around a mouthful.

"I love baking. It totally relaxes me, and the finished product is always so yummy."

"You can bake for me any time."

They stared at each other, letting those words settle between them. Shy smiles split both their mouths, then Sarah brushed the crumbs off her hands, and slowly reached out a hand, wrapping it around Bethany's.

"This okay?" Sarah murmured.

"Yes," Bethany whispered, and squeezed Sarah's hand gently.

"Good," Sarah replied, her voice soft on the breeze.

They sat like that for some minutes, simply holding hands, looking down at the water, occasionally pointing out something of interest to each other but otherwise content to be quiet.

It was good, and Bethany knew without a doubt that on this date they'd moved past the worst. She hoped Sarah would be able to shake off her fears, but at least Bethany knew about them now.

Eventually, Sarah said, "I don't know about you, but I'm really starting to feel that sun on my skin. How about we head to a coffee shop I know near here, and get some shade?"

"Perfect."

They spent another hour in each other's company before Sarah took them the long way back through the park to show Bethany all the legacy buildings left over from 2012. Sarah itched to hold Bethany's hand the whole way but at the same time, didn't trust herself not to overdo it, or do the wrong thing entirely, so instead she walked close and simply enjoyed being in Bethany's presence. The afternoon had been so good, she didn't want to risk anything spoiling it—for once, she wanted to walk away from a date with Bethany with a smile on her face.

Their goodbye was said outside Stratford station, where they were headed for different Tube lines.

"You know," Sarah said quietly as they stood to one side, tucked around the corner from the station concourse, away from the crowds. "I had a wonderful day with you, Bethany."

Bethany smiled widely. "Me too."

Sarah mulled over what to do next. Would kissing Bethany goodbye be too much too soon? She sighed, and settled for asking, "Can we get together during the week?"

"I'd like that. Shall I call you tomorrow, make some plans?"

"Perfect."

They stared at each other. There was a lovely tension between them, one that Sarah was finding hard to resist. She was surprised, but in a good way, when Bethany suddenly stepped in to her space, tilted her head up, and dropped a soft, brief kiss on Sarah's lips. Even though it was momentary, the touch was electric.

"Bethany," Sarah whispered, her eyes wide. Then she made to reach out, but stopped herself.

"What?" Bethany asked softly.

"This will sound odd, but I'm worried if I return that kiss I'll take things too far. Get carried away and say or do something stupid."

Bethany smiled and shook her head.

"I'm serious," Sarah insisted. "I just…don't want to rush it. You see"— she swallowed—"if I rush it, I'll probably do to you what I did to all the others."

"Which is what?"

Sarah sighed. "Never call you again," she said, her voice only just above a whisper as the shame swept over her. Saying it like that, confessing it to someone as wonderful as Bethany, made Sarah feel like a total shit.

"I see." Bethany cleared her throat and stepped back a little. "Just how many other women have there been? Or don't I want to know the answer to that?"

"You probably don't," Sarah admitted.

"Right." There was a pause, and then Bethany tilted her head. "So, are you clean? Health-wise, I mean."

Sarah nearly choked. She was still getting used to Bethany's penchant for asking direct questions.

"Er, yes, yes I am. I am regularly tested, and I practice safe sex with all my partners."

"Good. Because if we are going to sleep together, you will be my first sexual partner in some time, and I really wouldn't want any additional… souvenirs from the experience."

Sarah snorted before she could stop herself but just as she made to apologise, Bethany laughed, putting her at ease. "I definitely wouldn't want to do that to you, Bethany."

"Thank you." Bethany's voice was quiet.

Sarah's curiosity got the better of her. "Can I ask, how long, exactly, has it been for you?"

Bethany sighed. "I don't want to admit it, but you have been honest with me, so… It's nearly seven years."

Holy shit.

"Oh." Sarah stared at her.

"Changed your mind?" The smile on Bethany's face was teasing.

"No! Not at all. I just…" Sarah laughed. "God, for the first time in ages I'm actually feeling nervous about sex." And she was—talk about pressure to please. If Bethany had had no one touch her in seven years, Sarah would feel the need to make it extra special for her, to make up for all that lost time.

"Why would you be nervous? I'm the one who hasn't done it in ages. Mind you, like I told you already, I *do* know what I want. You don't have to worry about me being completely clueless, you know."

Sarah's eyes widened. "You astound me."

"Why?"

"Because you're so bold about this. You come across as shy in so many ways, and yet in others, you just throw it right out there. It's kind of awesome and scary all at the same time."

Bethany huffed out an extended breath and shuffled her feet. "Sarah, the seven years of celibacy was right for me, and I don't regret it. But now, I know I want something more, and I know that you are the first woman in a long time who has stirred those feelings in me. So I want to go for it. Trust me, I'm quaking inside at this entire conversation, but I won't let that stop me."

"Wow." Sarah didn't know what else to say. Determined Bethany was damn sexy.

"Now, back to the concept of not rushing," Bethany said, her tone brisk and business like.

"Yeah?"

Bethany leaned in, the warmth of her tantalisingly close. "Don't leave me waiting too long, Sarah." Her voice was a little lower than normal, and definitely huskier.

"Okay," Sarah croaked out as all the blood in her body migrated towards her clit.

Bethany kissed her once more, lingering a little longer this time, then stepped back.

"I'll call you tomorrow, okay?"

"Uh-huh." Sarah was left in a daze, but it was a really, *really* good place to be.

Bethany flopped into a seat on the train, her heart racing and her hands trembling. It had been a wonderful afternoon, and finally getting to really know Sarah had settled her doubts about whether it was worth pursuing something with her or not.

But it was the last ten minutes that had particularly taken her breath away.

Had she been body-snatched? Who had taken her over and allowed her to talk so freely to Sarah about s-e-x? Yes, Bethany *did* know what she wanted when it came to physical pleasure with another woman—she'd spent the last year or so carefully thinking that through, being honest with herself about where her desires lay. But to actually talk to Sarah about it, and—good Lord—tell her not to wait too long before taking Bethany to her bed?

Bethany smiled, puffing out her cheeks with a big breath. Of course, if she was really feeling bold, she wouldn't wait for Sarah to do the taking. After all, wasn't that part of where her desires were driving her? Being the one to take charge—set the pace, have the control?

She grinned. Sarah had seemed flabbergasted at this new side of her, and she had to admit, catching the cool and composed Sarah out like that had felt good.

Bethany wondered how many other, far more interesting ways she could find to disassemble Sarah Connolly.

CHAPTER 13

"So, dear, tonight is the night, yes?" Evelyn's tone was hard to read. "You are going on another date with Bethany."

"I am," Sarah said, tucking her phone under her chin and reaching for the shirt she'd hung up earlier that evening when she'd been pondering just what to wear for her momentous date with Bethany.

She had persuaded Bethany to let this be her treat—no splitting the bill tonight. Sarah wanted to spoil Bethany; make her feel special. Not to show off, or flash her cash—which it was obvious Sarah had much more of—but simply to treat her to things she probably didn't get the chance to enjoy very often.

If she wasn't careful, she'd be late. However, when Evelyn called, Sarah always answered—she owed her aunt too much to let her go to voicemail. And, she had to be honest, there was always that tinge of fear when Evelyn called—would she hear her aunt crying for help after a fall, or a stroke, or something equally awful? Sarah knew it was irrational, especially with Jonathan in the house most of the day, but Sarah always did the 'what if' where her beloved aunt was concerned. What if, in the hour or so it took Jonathan to go to Tesco for the weekly groceries, or on one of his nights off, something happened? Not for the first time, Sarah wondered if she should have moved in with Evelyn when she'd offered a room all those years ago.

Yeah, but if you'd done that, just imagine how much it would have cramped your style over the years. And you'd have ended up resenting Evelyn as a result.

She shook her head, focusing back on her aunt's voice.

"Are you looking forward to it?"

"Of course! I'm rather excited actually."

"Hm."

"What?" Sarah stopped trying to wrestle herself into the shirt and stood upright. "What does 'hm' mean?"

Evelyn sighed. "Forgive me, dear. I am simply a tad concerned at this new version of you. Whether it is really what is good for you. You have spent so much time avoiding relationships, it is somewhat of a turnaround for you to be throwing yourself so wholeheartedly into this one."

Sarah sighed, and sat down on the edge of the bed. "Evelyn, I love you. You know that, right?"

"Of course, dear."

"And I know you're only concerned about me, and that this is your way of trying to protect me, yes?"

"Indeed."

"Okay. But you have to trust me on this. You really do. Bethany is so very different from all the other women I've been with, and that's why I am so attracted to her, I think. And why I'm sticking my neck out into uncharted territory. She's a wonderful woman, Evelyn. She's got a brain, for one thing, and isn't afraid to use it. Plus there's something so sexy about her complete lack of awareness of how sexy she is. She...intrigues me. And *that* excites me."

"All right, all right." Evelyn's tone was resigned. "It does sound like you have given this some thought."

"I have. Now, I'm sorry, but I need to go and get ready."

Evelyn was quiet for a moment. "Please be careful, Sarah. I do not want to see you get hurt."

"I promise I'll look after myself, okay?"

"Thank you, dear. I will talk to you soon."

"I'll call you tomorrow, okay?"

"Only if you have time."

"I'll make time, Evelyn. Always, for you."

Evelyn chuckled. "Sweet talker," she said. "Goodbye."

"Bye, Evelyn."

Sarah was smiling as she tossed the phone on the bed, but that smile faded as she thought back on Evelyn's words. Her aunt's doubts swirled around her mind, mixing with her own nerves. Uncharted territory indeed. But she certainly wasn't going to chicken out now, especially when the alternative was *not* seeing Bethany again. Sarah had prided herself on her courage throughout her life, with, she could admit, one or two lapses when things got particularly hairy. However, she'd stuck to her guns in all sorts of scenarios over the years, following her gut instinct to get what she wanted from life.

And, lately, it seemed she wanted Bethany.

Bethany, who drew Sarah to her in ways that she couldn't begin to fathom, or fight.

So I'm not going to fight it.

She stood up and finished buttoning up the shirt. It was one of her favourites, a deep burgundy colour and with a shape that fit her body like a glove. Paired with smart black trousers and a black leather jacket, it was a classy yet sexy look. One she hoped Bethany would appreciate.

She checked her make-up one more time, teased a few strands of hair back into position, and pulled on the leather jacket. Staring at her reflection in the long mirror next to the dresser, she found her smile again.

Alice swept into the flat, a garment bag draped over her arms.

"Hello, love. Sorry I'm a bit late. The bus got held up. Some idiot tried to jump on through the back doors and the driver wouldn't move until he'd got off and got back on again at the front." She tutted. "What a plonker."

Bethany laughed, showing her mum into the living room. "No worries; there's plenty of time."

"There is? Oh, thank God. I didn't want to be the one responsible for mucking up your big date." Alice dropped the garment bag on the back of the sofa, then turned to look at Bethany, her hands on her hips. "So, how are you feeling?"

Bethany grinned. "Nervous. Excited. I looked the restaurant up online—I don't think I've ever been anywhere so posh."

"Ooh, this is so exciting!" Alice stepped across the room and pulled her into a quick hug. "Your make-up looks gorgeous, by the way."

"Thanks, Mum."

"Now, here it is," Alice said, gesturing towards the garment bag. "Want to get into it right now?"

Bethany nodded and her mum smiled. When she pulled the dress from its cover, Bethany's eyes misted over.

The dress was just above knee-length, and had a retro early sixties feel, with a wide skirt and cinched-in waist. Made of a green satin material with pink flourishes around the waist and hemline, it had been Alice's when she was a young woman.

"Last time I wore this, your dad proposed to me," Alice said, her voice quiet as she held the dress up. "One of the happiest days of my life."

Bethany's throat closed up. When her mum had offered the dress, she'd had no idea of its importance.

"Oh, Mum. Are you sure you want me to wear it tonight? What if I spill something on it?"

Alice waved off her protests, eyes shining with unshed tears. "You'll be fine. And yes, I would love you to wear this. I've always thought it would suit you. Maybe that's why I held onto it all these years."

She cupped Bethany's face in her hands. "This is a very special night for you, I know that. So you need a special dress." She stepped back. "Come on, try it on. I reckon you'll look smashing in it. I'll pop the kettle on for a quick cuppa while you do."

Her mum stepped into the kitchen and moments later Bethany heard her making the promised beverage.

Bethany took the dress to her bedroom, where it took only a minute to disrobe, then step into the dress, ease it up over her hips, and zip up the back. She admired herself in the mirror on the inside of the wardrobe door before her mum's light footsteps on the wooden floor of the hallway broke her out of her uncustomary self-appreciation.

"You can come in," Bethany called. "I'm decent."

Her mum pushed open the door and gasped as Bethany twirled in front of her. Alice had been right—she did look smashing. The colours in the dress worked incredibly well with Bethany's often nondescript hair colour and style, and the cut of it suited her body shape to a tee.

"Oh, Bethany. You look fantastic!" Alice stared at her, eyes wide.

"I love it!" Bethany enthused as she twirled once more.

"Good. And I'm sure Sarah will love it too."

Bethany blushed. "I hope so."

"You really like this woman, don't you?" Alice asked, taking hold of Bethany's arm and bringing her twirling to a stop.

"Yes, I really do."

"And are you sure you can trust her?"

Bethany tilted her head. "Mum?"

Alice sighed, rubbing her hand up and down Bethany's arm. "I'll trust your judgement, love, but..."

"You think she'll muck me around again?"

"I hope she doesn't. I really do." Alice smiled wanly. "It's your life, Bethany. You go out and live it how you choose. I just don't want to see you get hurt, that's all."

Bethany gave her mum a quick hug. "I know. I understand." She grinned. "It is kind of lovely and scary all at the same time—I can't lie about that. After spending so long on my own, it's hard to believe that I've met someone so quickly who makes me feel this way, but..." She shrugged. "I know we had a bit of a bumpy start, but it seems to be working now, so I'm just going to go with the flow."

Alice gave her a gentle pat on the shoulder. "Good for you, love. It's lovely to see you this excited about being with someone. I..." She pulled back and gazed into Bethany's eyes. "I did worry, for a little while. You know, that you'd be on your own. I mean, if that was what you truly wanted then obviously I would have been supportive, but somehow I wasn't sure it really was."

Bethany hugged her mother again. "You know, it actually *was* what I wanted, for a while, and I was okay with that. But now I'm not, so here I am." She let go of her mother and spread her arms wide, grinning like an idiot.

Alice laughed, and shook her head. "You're fifteen all over again, and I think it's lovely."

Bethany smiled and walked over to where she had left the shoes she'd picked out to go with the dress. They were heeled, a rarity for her, and strappy, and ridiculously *not* sensible, but she'd been unable to resist pulling them from the back of her wardrobe. Once her feet were firmly buckled in, she walked carefully over to the mirror once more, adjusting to the feel of the shoes, the way she needed to alter her gait slightly to walk in them properly.

"Lovely," Alice said, catching Bethany's eye in the mirror. "Just lovely."

"Thanks, Mum."

She took the Tube to Leicester Square and followed Sarah's instructions to the pedestrianised side road that was home to J Sheekey's, one of the best—if not *the* best—fish and seafood restaurants in London. Bethany knew it was sought after, and pricey, and Sarah treating her to this put a lovely squishy feeling in her stomach.

The doorman pulled open the door with a pleasant "Good evening" and Bethany stepped into the cosy interior. The hostess showed her to the table, where she found Sarah waiting. A thrill shot through her at the open-mouthed stare Sarah sent her way; Sarah's gaze roamed over every inch of Bethany's body, and goose bumps erupted over every one of those inches.

"Hello," Bethany said, suddenly feeling shy under such obvious scrutiny.

"Bethany," Sarah breathed, her eyes wide. "You look...stunning."

"Thank you." Bethany ducked her head, her cheeks flaming. Being complimented like that would take some getting used to.

She sat down in the chair the hostess pulled out for her and waited until her napkin had been draped across her lap before raising her head again. Sarah was still staring, and smiling, and Bethany chuckled.

"Earth to Sarah," she said.

Sarah blinked a few times, grinning. "Sorry." She shook her head. "No, actually, I'm not sorry." She reached across the table and took Bethany's hand. "You are beautiful, Bethany. Thank you for this." She waved in a motion that encompassed Bethany's body. "Simply incredible."

"Thank you," Bethany whispered, almost overwhelmed with emotion.

And not just because of the words themselves, but the way they were delivered—with intensity and...passion—had Bethany's temperature rising and her heart racing. She squeezed Sarah's hand, then let go and reached for her menu. She needed something to do; something to distract her before she lunged across the table and kissed Sarah senseless. She looked positively edible tonight. The burgundy shirt totally suited her colouring, and she'd ruffled her hair slightly and applied some smoky make-up to her eyes, giving her a come-to-bed look that Bethany would willingly take her up on, given half a chance.

"Everything here is wonderful," Sarah said softly. "So please order whatever you wish."

"Thank you." Bethany met her gaze. "And thank you in advance for treating me. This already feels amazing and I haven't eaten or drunk anything yet."

Sarah smiled, and they gazed at each other for a few seconds before a discreet cough from the waiter snapped them out of their reverie.

"Ladies, would you like to order some drinks?"

After they'd decided on a bottle of Pinot Blanc and ordered a mouth-watering array of food—and agreed to sample each other's starters and mains so they could appreciate all the flavours on offer—Sarah lifted her glass.

"To you, for being here tonight. Thank you."

Bethany blushed. "And to you, for arranging all of this. Thank you."

They delicately clinked glasses, then sipped at the wine.

"Oh my God, that's *good*." Bethany took another sip, and Sarah smiled at her across the top of her own glass.

"So, nearly finished with term?"

"Yes! Don't get me wrong, I love the kids in my class, but I cannot wait for summer holidays to start."

Sarah laughed. "And here I was thinking you were super dedicated to your work, to the cause of education in this country."

"I am!" Bethany smirked. "But I'm also a tired human being who needs a break."

"Do you have any plans for your time off?"

"Well, the first week will be spent sleeping a lot."

Sarah laughed.

"The second week I'm away with my mum, down in Cornwall, visiting my Aunt Mary, one of my dad's sisters."

Sarah tilted her head. "You and your mum are visiting one of your dad's sisters? Why isn't your dad coming too?"

It still hurt, even after all these years, to say the words out loud.

"Oh, my dad died. When I was nine. But my mum has kept us in touch with all of his family and we see them often."

Sarah eyes had widened. "I'm sorry."

Bethany shrugged and smiled. "You weren't to know. It's okay. Besides, seeing his sisters always reminds me of him, so it's almost like he's there with us. We have the most fantastic time with them—with Aunt Mary in particular. The three of us love spending time together, so I'm really looking forward to it. And I love Cornwall, so that's a nice bonus."

"Wow, you're actually excited about spending time with your mum and aunt?" Sarah looked bemused.

Bethany tilted her head. "Do you think that's strange?"

"Um, no. Not really, I guess. Sorry, I think I must be projecting my own feelings about family onto your situation, which is silly. It sounds like you're close to yours."

"Oh, very! I have a big family, and we all get on like a house on fire. I gather that's not the same for you?" She dared the question, but was ready to tell Sarah to ignore it if it was obvious that it was too much.

Sarah looked away briefly. When her gaze returned, there was a sadness in her eyes that made Bethany's stomach squirm.

"It's… I was adopted," Sarah blurted. She blinked a couple of times before adding, "Sorry, I don't normally just throw that out there."

"Oh." Bethany was flummoxed. Should she ask Sarah more about it or shut up and change the subject? She'd never met anyone who'd been adopted, at least not to her knowledge. What was the etiquette?

Sarah sighed. "So, my birth mother gave me up for adoption when I was about two years old. I don't remember her, and I have no idea who my dad was. I'm not even sure my mother knew. She…she was a sex worker, you see. Apparently she tried to raise me as best she could, but money was always a problem with a small kid in tow, as were unscrupulous landlords, and in the end, it all got too much."

Bethany reached across the table and took Sarah's hand in her own.

"My adoptive parents are lovely people, but it seems they never intended me to know I was adopted." Sarah's eyes lost their focus; she was clearly lost in memories. "I…I was a bit of a handful when I was a teenager, and one night, when they were out at a dinner party and had trusted me to look after myself at home for the evening, I went…snooping. To this day I'm not really sure why I did." She chuckled. "Well, I know part of it—I couldn't figure out how my parents were so rich when my mum didn't work and my dad didn't seem to work that hard either." She snorted softly. "So I broke into my dad's study and had a good rummage through all his paperwork. Didn't take me long to find my file."

Her eyes had taken on a haunted look, and Bethany squeezed her hand harder, giving Sarah an anchor if she needed it. Sarah reached for her wine with her free hand and took a long sip.

"Anyway, I confronted them when they came home; the truth all came out, and for about a year afterwards, things were decidedly rocky between us. We went to a family counsellor, and that did help. I was angry, of course—angry at being given up by my mother, and angry at them for keeping it from me. Now, as an adult, I can see why they made the choices they did—all of them. But at fourteen, none of that was clear."

"I can imagine," Bethany murmured.

Sarah shrugged. "So, I'm sorry. Family for me is always a sore spot. My parents and I are now at a reasonably good place together, but there's always…something. Something making me feel like I don't quite belong. I mean, don't get me wrong, my adoptive parents love me. Wholeheartedly. It's my issue, and I've never quite got on top of it."

Sarah's fingers squeezed Bethany's, then let go as the waiter appeared with their starters. When he had finished laying the plates down and backed away, Sarah said, "Sorry, I didn't mean to bring something so serious into our evening."

"No! It's fine. I… Thank you for telling me. I know that probably wasn't easy."

"Not many people know that about me," Sarah said, shaking her head slowly. "Somehow I just needed you to know, I guess."

"Thank you. I'm honoured you felt you could share that with me."

Sarah nodded, and they each picked up their cutlery to dig into their starters—dressed crab for Sarah, and scallops for Bethany. They moaned in appreciation at the flavours, then immediately offered samples to each other.

After a couple more mouthfuls, Sarah sipped her wine again, then said, "And, hey, it's not all bad—I have a wonderful aunt, Evelyn, who is my adoptive father's older sister. We became very close from as early as I can remember." She smiled. "She's an amazing woman, and she helped me out a lot when my history all got revealed. I would often spend days at her place, listening to her raucous stories of all the amazing parties she'd gone to in the sixties. She was quite the socialite, I think, and knew a lot of famous people."

"She sounds wonderful."

"Oh, she is. She's outspoken, feisty, and I love her to bits. She never married, and she's got some story there that I'll get out of her one day." She chuckled. "Evelyn's helped me out of some difficult times, and I am so grateful she's in my life."

"Do you see her often?"

"Oh, God, yes! Like, at least twice a week. She still lives in this big house in Mile End, one of those gorgeous Georgian terraces, you know?"

Bethany nodded, entranced.

"She's in her eighties now, and a little bit slower than she used to be, so she has this live-in carer, Jonathan. He's been with her over ten years so he's not really an employee anymore, more like an adopted son. They treat each other like shit sometimes, but they do make me laugh—they're inseparable. God knows what they'll do when Jonathan finally meets the man of his dreams and wants to settle down." She sipped her wine. "Mind you, he'd probably just move his man in there and the pair of them would look after her."

"You love her very much, I can tell. Your face lights up talking about her." It gave Bethany such joy to see that in Sarah after what she'd said about her adoptive parents.

"I do, that is very true." Sarah shook her head, smiling in bewilderment. "How did you do that? I never talk to anyone about my family, and now I've just told you all of it."

Bethany's heart pounded. "I guess, or at least I hope, it means you feel comfortable enough with me to be able to talk about your life like that. And that you know, on some level, that you can trust me with it."

Sarah stared at her, then reached across the table to hold her hand. "Yes," she said, her voice husky. "All of that."

Moments after the waiter had cleared their starter plates away, Sarah excused herself to the bathroom. Confessing her family history to Bethany had not been on the agenda, though it had felt strangely good talking about that painful part of her life. But now her feelings were…raw, and she needed to pull herself together so she could really enjoy the rest of the evening.

When she returned to the table, Bethany was gazing appreciatively around the room. "This really is a beautiful place," she said. "Have you seen how many famous faces are in the photos on the walls?"

Sarah smiled at the almost childlike enthusiasm. "I know, it's very cool. I love it here."

"So," Bethany whispered, leaning forward until her face was only inches away, "is this where you bring all your women?"

Sarah flinched before she saw the twinkle in Bethany's eyes. God, this woman…

"Oh yeah," Sarah said, playing along. "Yep, wine them and dine them, then take them home and have my wicked way with them."

Bethany flushed bright pink but leaned even closer. "Well," she murmured, "this is our fourth date, after all. Third date was the sex date, right? So we're way behind schedule, and you owe me."

Sarah hung her head in defeat. Game, set, and match to Bethany.

"Oh God, woman, you're going to kill me. Seriously."

Bethany laughed, and Sarah laughed along with her, delighting in their interaction. Everything about Bethany was easy yet challenging, exciting yet strangely calming. Sarah wasn't quite herself when she was around Bethany, but it didn't alarm her. In fact, she positively revelled in it.

"We could, you know." Bethany's voice was quiet, and Sarah only just picked up her words.

"Could what?"

"Go home together. Tonight." Bethany's eyes were wide, her cheeks still a little pink, but there was a heated desire in her expression that had Sarah's breath catching in her already constricted throat.

"Are…are you serious?" she squeaked.

"Ladies," the waiter said, placing two plates of steaming food in front of them, "your mains."

CHAPTER 14

BETHANY WAITED UNTIL THEIR MEALS had been served, and the waiter had departed, before she dared to speak again. She was feeling a strange mix of bold and nervous, and it was tying her stomach in knots. Which wasn't the best feeling to have when a plate of delicious-looking sea bass had just been placed in front of her.

Hoping her voice wouldn't croak, she leaned in and said, "Yes, I am serious. If you still think it's too soon, and would like some more time, then of course I will wait. But I meant what I said last Saturday—you don't have to go slow on my account. Not anymore."

She smiled as Sarah's mouth dropped open, and leaned further forward to place a finger firmly underneath her chin, popping it closed again.

"I want you, Sarah. I just wanted to make that clear."

And oh my, how she did want her. Sarah looked so good tonight, and the intimate conversation had only deepened their connection. The way Sarah had let a little of her vulnerability show through that confident exterior spread a warmth through Bethany's chest. And simmering nicely in the back of her mind were fantasies of how much she'd like to unravel Sarah, delve beneath that sometimes hard shell to find out just how soft she was when it got stripped away.

Sarah was staring at her, and Bethany saw her swallow before responding. "Bethany, you... I love how you don't hold back. It's intoxicating."

Sarah blushed, and Bethany swelled with pride. She'd done that.

"This is going to take some getting used to," Sarah continued, shaking her head and chuckling softly.

"What?"

"Being outplayed." Sarah grinned sheepishly.

Bethany laughed, that feeling of pride extending beyond her chest to every part of her body. "Well, I have no plans to stop—so yes, you do need to get used to it."

Inside she was a bag of nerves, but outside she knew she was projecting a calm and confident poise. There was something about being with Sarah, especially since their picnic last week. Something Bethany couldn't begin to identify, but that both gave her an outlet for her innermost wishes—to take the lead, to be the one bringing her partner to her knees with desire, to act as if she knew exactly what she was doing—and, at the same time, had her dreading she'd chicken out when they finally did make it to a bedroom. Or that Sarah would exert her natural confidence in the bedroom as well as she did in settings such as the sex shop where they'd met. That wouldn't necessarily mean Bethany wouldn't enjoy herself, she was sure. But she was so ready to act on her fantasies that she felt like a firework on a very short fuse.

Sarah shook her head and picked up her fork. "I think I'd better eat this." She gestured at her dish of monkfish and tiger prawns. "Partly to give me a breather from this charged atmosphere." She smirked at Bethany. "And partly because it sounds like I may need some energy later."

Bethany swallowed hard as her clit leaped to attention.

Sarah placed her hand in the small of Bethany's back as they passed through the door from the restaurant to the street. Her touch was warm even through the fabric of the dress, making Bethany's skin tingle.

Every word, every touch since Bethany's bold statement had been this electrifying. And she was quite sure she wasn't the only one affected that way. Sarah had worn a somewhat dazed look the entire time they'd eaten their mains, and they hadn't had that much to drink, so Bethany knew the wine wasn't to blame.

She turned to smile at Sarah, and the heat in Sarah's eyes nearly made her falter. Could she do this? Suddenly the practicalities of having her first sex in seven years set her heart pounding. Her body—her *naked* body—was about to go on display in front of someone else. She'd kept up with a personal grooming regime for a while now, so that element wasn't contributing greatly to her nerves. But the thought of all of her being exposed, and someone else's equally bare body presented before her, had her quivering. Was it nerves or excitement?

"Bethany?" Sarah's voice broke into her thoughts. "Are you okay?"

"Um, yes. I'm fine."

Sarah tilted her head. "I was talking to you, but you looked sort of out of it."

Bethany flushed. "Oh God, sorry! I… Yes, I drifted off for a few moments there. I'm so sorry." Her words came out in a rush and she clamped her lips shut to stop the flow.

Sarah stepped closer, the street lamp casting a soft orange glow on her dark hair. "Are you sure you're okay?" She rubbed a thumb over the back of Bethany's hand. "You know, we don't have to do this tonight. It's okay."

Bethany closed her eyes and took a breath. *Come on, get a grip!*

"I have to admit," she said, her voice catching slightly, "I am a little nervous, I think. I mean, I'm excited too, but, you know, it has been a while."

And I have a desire that I want to express but I don't know if it's something you would want, and I have no idea how to start that conversation.

"Maybe I am being a bit hasty." She dropped her head. *Ugh, this is all going wrong.*

Why couldn't she just go through with it? If she let her worries keep getting in the way, she'd never find out if she could have what she wanted. And she wanted Sarah—that much was certain.

Sarah stepped back. "Then we'll wait," she said, smiling encouragingly. "I said it before, and I meant it—I don't need to rush this. Not with you."

Bethany wrung her hands together. "I know, but I really want this." She snorted out a laugh. "Being this forthright with you, and saying all those things I said over dinner—I mean them, and I do feel all that. But now, standing out here"—she gestured at the bustling little street—"knowing we just need to get on the Tube together to make all of that real, I suddenly feel as if I am paralysed. It's embarrassing."

"Oh, hey. No, it's not," Sarah whispered, moving close again and wrapping her arms slowly and carefully around Bethany's waist.

The circle of Sarah's arms grounded her, and the warmth of her embrace sent shivers skittering across Bethany's exposed skin.

"And," she whispered in Bethany's ear, "I'm nervous too." She leaned back slightly so their eyes met. "You're the first woman I've allowed this close to me in years, and I don't want to do anything to push you away. I like what we have going on. I don't want anything to spoil that, and like I keep saying, there's no way I want to rush you into something you're not ready for." She chuckled. "And believe me, that's something I never thought *I'd* be saying."

Bethany squeezed Sarah tight, relishing the sensation of her body pressed so close, her breathing soft and gentle in front of Bethany's lips. "We're a pair, aren't we?"

Sarah laughed, nuzzling Bethany's nose with her own. "Yep, we are. But we'll get there. Don't worry. And when we do, that's when it will be right. Okay?"

"Sarah," Bethany murmured, noticing how little flecks shimmered in her brown eyes in the light from the street lamp.

"Yes?"

"Kiss me."

Sarah moaned softly, but it carried a depth of emotion that belied its volume. Without hesitating, she pressed her lips against Bethany's, and moments later their mouths parted and their tongues met. The kiss was long, and deep, and Bethany's heart rate soared as exquisite sensations washed over her in response. She pulled Sarah even closer, kissing her with an intensity she couldn't have tempered if she'd tried.

"Jeez, get a room, girls!"

The words, shouted from somewhere behind Sarah, were followed by the cackle of many voices laughing, although not nastily. Sarah and Bethany pulled apart, blushing, and then joined in the laughter as the group of young women passed.

"Think that's our cue to go home?" Sarah asked, her fingers stroking a delicate path down one of Bethany's cheeks to her jawline.

"Probably." Bethany shuffled on the spot. "I had a wonderful evening. Thank you."

Sarah nodded enthusiastically. "Me too. Very much so."

"Can I...can I call you later, when I get in? Just to say goodnight?"

Did that sound pathetic?

"I'd like that. A lot," Sarah said, beaming.

Bethany sighed with relief. "Great. Okay, so I'm going that way." She pointed behind Sarah at Leicester Square in the distance.

"And I'm going that way." Sarah pointed in the opposite direction. She leaned forward and kissed Bethany, gently this time, her lips soft and slow. "Get home safe," she whispered as she pulled back again.

Sarah pushed the door to her flat closed behind her and leaned back against it, shaking her head and laughing to herself.

What an evening. Bethany continued to surprise her, continued to fill every one of Sarah's senses with her presence and energy. Walking across the open-plan room to the kitchen area, Sarah dropped her handbag on the counter. She pulled out her phone and tucked it in her trouser pocket, then opened the fridge, reaching for a bottle of water.

It was a sticky night, and she moved to the balcony after slugging down two large mouthfuls of water. Out on the decking, she gazed down at the dark water below her. Limehouse Basin itself was quiet, the only sounds being those of cables clinking against boat masts in the gentle evening breeze, and occasional soft splashes in the water. A couple of flats across the way from hers had music playing, but not that loud; the sound simply carried across the water easier than it would have on a busy street. She sipped her water, her gaze unfocused as she thought back over the evening.

Her phone beeped, and she quickly pulled it out.

It was a text message from Jonathan, and she grinned as she read it.

I don't care what time you get home, CALL me and tell me everything xx

She hit the call icon and he answered on the first ring.

"Before you say anything, is she there with you now?" he said, words tumbling over each other in their rush to be heard.

"No!" she replied, aghast. "If she was do you think I'd be calling you?"

"Well, okay. Fair point." He gasped. "Wait, seriously? You didn't bring her home? Or go home with her?"

"Nope," Sarah said, grinning.

"Oh my, who *are* you, and what have you done with Sarah?"

She laughed. "This is a new era. A new me."

A thrill shot through her at those words. She did feel new, and it felt great.

"Colour me impressed," he said. "Wait, I need wine for this."

She heard the sounds of him opening a bottle, the muted pop of the cork unmistakeable even down a phone line, then the sound of liquid sloshing into a glass.

"There," he said, slurping, "that's better."

"Comfy now, are we?"

"Perfectly," he said. "Your aunt's in bed. Tell me *everything*."

Sarah guffawed, then sipped her water before launching into a description of how the evening had unfolded.

"Oh. My. God. You told her about your *parents*?"

"I know! Trust me, I never thought *that* was on the menu tonight."

"Wow. I mean, just, *wow*."

"Listen, I'm almost as shocked about this as you are. But, you know what? This, whatever this is between me and Bethany, is making me really happy. *Really* happy."

Jonathan sniffed.

"Oh, crap," Sarah said. "You're not crying, are you?"

"I might be," came a small voice, accompanied by more sniffles.

"Oh, Jonathan…"

"Oh, just ignore me. It's hormones or something."

"I feel…light," she whispered. "And happy. And I can't seem to stop smiling."

She grinned again, gazing out at the calming water below, her heart swelling with sensations she couldn't put a name to.

"You know, Sarah," Jonathan's voice was now very serious, "I am so impressed you were able to hold back your usual tendency to rush the physical side of things."

She chuckled and exhaled a long breath. "Yep. I mean, don't get me wrong, it wasn't easy, especially when she made it clear she was more than willing to hit the fast-forward button."

"Really? I assumed these primary school teachers were all quiet and demure."

134

"Hah! Not this one, trust me." Sarah lost focus for a moment as images of Bethany leaning across the table to proposition her swept into her mind. "But I just knew waiting was the right thing to do." She shook her head. "Still can't believe I did though."

"I am so proud of you, you know. And thank you, that was an excellent progress report."

She laughed. "You're welcome. Tell me, is this a new thing? Do I need to report back after every date?"

"Possibly." Jonathan sniggered. "Depends on what your next step is."

"My next step is to wait for her to call me in a while, once she's home. She wanted…" Oh God, how much was he going to rib her if she admitted *this*? "She wanted to call me to say goodnight."

"Oh, that's it. I'm done. Pass me the Kleenex."

He made exaggerated sobbing noises in her ear and she snorted with laughter.

"Fuck off. I'll talk to you soon."

"You will, darling. Say hi to Bethany for me!"

Shaking her head, she ended the call and put the phone down on the small table on the deck. She had just finished her bottle of water when it rang, and she smiled when she saw Bethany's number appear in the caller display.

"Hey, you."

"Hey, you got home okay?" Bethany sounded breathless, and Sarah wondered if she'd literally just walked through her front door.

"I sure did. And you?"

"Yes, no problems."

"Good." Sarah chuckled. "I just got off the phone with Jonathan. He wanted a progress report. And he says hi, by the way."

"Aw, that's sweet. But, progress report?"

Sarah groaned but she was smiling. "Yes. Let me tell you all about Jonathan…"

CHAPTER 15

SARAH IDLY STIRRED HER COFFEE as she leaned her chin on her free hand. She had no idea how long she'd been gazing out the window of Starbucks, and frankly didn't care. Thoughts of Bethany, of that kiss on Saturday night, of the spectacular dress Bethany had worn and how bloody beautiful she was, consumed her. She'd walked around in a daze since that night with a big grin on her face that she wouldn't wipe off, even if she could. She chuckled to herself, and took another sip of her latte.

"Well," said a voice, "wherever you were looked wonderful."

It was Scott, standing next to her and beaming his wide smile.

Sarah laughed, blushing. "Yeah, you know, it actually was."

Scott held up a finger. "Hold that thought. Let me get a coffee and then I want to know what's put that dreamy expression on your face." His face fell. "Wait, that was pretty presumptuous of me, wasn't it? I mean, we don't know each other that well and—"

"I'd love to talk," Sarah cut in. "Go get your coffee."

He grinned and strode off towards the counter.

It was a shock to realise, but she really did want to share this with him. Hell, she'd share it with anybody right now, she was so happy. Nervous still, of course, and feeling a tad out of her depth, but she couldn't wait to gush about Saturday night to her new acquaintance—a man who had every chance of becoming a friend, based on their previous interactions.

"So," he said when he returned and perched on the stool opposite hers. "That's twice now I've caught you lost in your own little world, but this one seemed a much happier place."

Sarah grinned. "I've started seeing someone. Her name is Bethany and she's…incredible."

"Yes!" Scott fist-pumped. "Okay, let me live vicariously. How many dates? Where have you been? What's she like?"

It took twenty minutes to fill him in. She glossed over some of her less-than-charming early behaviour, but at the same time didn't shy away from what trouble it had caused.

"God, I'm seriously impressed," Scott said when she'd finished. He chugged his coffee. "And also completely envious, obviously." His grin was wide, but his eyes were sad.

"So what's your ideal partner got to have, and why haven't you found him yet?"

Scott sighed. "Someone well balanced, who knows who they are and what they want. Someone who believes in monogamy and honesty. Rich and handsome would be a big bonus." He grinned. "But actually, neither of those are important." He leaned forward onto his folded arms. "And I haven't found him yet because, well, I suppose I don't help myself. I don't want to do the club scene, and even if I did I'm hardly likely to meet my type there. But something about using online dating makes my skin crawl. I want to meet someone face-to-face, like you did with Bethany, and get to know them gradually. Although," he said with a wry smile, "I'd like to think I'd make a better first attempt at talking with them than you did."

"Oi!" she retorted, but grinned as he laughed.

"Work doesn't help at the moment either," he continued. "I'm so busy I don't have much free time to think about my options. Like, it occurred to me maybe I could join some sort of social group around one of my interests, meet men that way. I like swimming. Maybe there's a gay swimming club?" he mused, his gaze drifting as he thought it through.

"What about getting set up with a friend of someone?" The question was out before she'd even thought about it, as if her sub-conscious had been dying to jump in. Now that she'd asked, it was so bloody obvious.

"Oh, no!" He held his hands up. "No, I've had way too many disasters with that."

"But he's really—"

"No. Sorry, Sarah, but no." His tone was firm, and she had to respect it even as her brain screamed that he and Jonathan wanted so many of the same things in life. Maybe there'd be a way she could engineer a meeting...

"You okay?" Scott asked. "You've drifted again."

She smiled, her mind working a mile a minute. "All good. Trust me."

"Looking forward to your last day at work before summer?" Sarah's low, warm voice sent exquisite shivers rippling over Bethany's body.

She had to clear her throat before speaking. "Oh yes. Like you wouldn't believe. I had two children throw up on me yesterday. I am very much ready for the break."

Bethany grinned as Sarah made gagging sounds. It was Thursday evening and they had been on the phone every night this week since their fantastic dinner date on Saturday. Sarah had been working long hours, so there had been no opportunity to see each other. On the one hand, Bethany welcomed the breathing space after the intensity of their last date, and the almost-sex they didn't have. On the other hand, talking to Sarah just before bedtime each night had been pure torture—imagining her face, and her body, hearing her soft voice whispering in Bethany's ear. All of it tormented her poor libido until she was a quivering mess of need and want at the end of each call.

The vibrator was certainly earning its keep this week.

"I honestly don't know how you do it," Sarah said, her tone full of wonder. "How do you just get on with that and sound so bloody cheerful about it?"

Bethany laughed. "It's just part of the territory. And to be fair, it's rare to have two in one day—sometimes I can go weeks without a vomit incident. The kids are usually pretty lovely to work with and I enjoy my days. And on days that I don't, I go home and bake something and that makes everything feel all right again."

"So how much did you bake after yesterday?" Sarah asked, chuckling.

"Two dozen raspberry muffins and a large batch of peanut butter cookies."

Sarah howled with laughter and Bethany's face ached from smiling so widely.

"I miss you," Sarah said suddenly, and Bethany's breath hitched in her throat. Sarah's voice was croaky as she added, "That's a new feeling for me."

"Oh," Bethany said, feeling a strange tingle sweep over her body. "I… That's lovely to hear. That you miss me. I miss you too."

"Are we still on for Saturday?"

"Definitely."

They had made arrangements for another afternoon together, this time at an art exhibition, with an understanding that the afternoon could well blend into the evening—and possibly into the next day? Bethany wished tomorrow was Saturday, wished she didn't have to go to work; that she could simply spend time with her girlfriend. The word popped easily into her mind, but *were* they girlfriends? Did you have to sleep together before you could call yourself that? She asked the question before she could second-guess herself.

"Are we exclusive, Sarah?"

Sarah hissed out a breath and Bethany's heart clenched in fear. She was pleasantly surprised when Sarah said, "Yes. I…I'm committed to this, Bethany. I won't lie and say I know exactly what I'm doing here, but yes, this is just you and me. I don't need anything else."

"Thank you, I really needed to hear that."

"Does my past worry you?"

Bethany sighed. "A little, yes."

Sarah was silent for a moment. "Thanks for being honest. I don't blame you for worrying. I think I would too if I was in your shoes. I will work very hard at earning your trust, Bethany."

"Just keep doing what you're doing," Bethany murmured. "It's all good so far."

"Good. I'm glad." Sarah huffed out a breath. "God, I really want to kiss you right now."

Bethany groaned. "Don't," she whispered. "I'm already dying here, don't make it any worse."

Sarah's throaty laugh sent shivers of desire up Bethany's thighs to their apex.

"Fair's fair," Sarah said. "I've been wet since you said you missed me."

The word 'wet' ricocheted around Bethany's brain, threatening to short-circuit her synapses. "Oh God," she breathed.

"Sorry, maybe that was a little too much too soon."

Sarah sounded genuinely contrite and Bethany rushed to mollify her. "No. God no! It was delicious. I love knowing I can do that to you."

"Oh, Bethany, you do. Trust me. You do."

"Why isn't it Saturday yet?" she whined, and Sarah laughed.

Sarah trotted down the steps at Limehouse station, her movements light and carefree. It was only six o'clock and she was already nearly home for the weekend. After pulling some serious hours all through the week, she'd wrapped up in good time to get out the door at five thirty. Her boss hadn't minded, simply waved at Sarah as she'd practically skipped out the office. Although she wasn't seeing Bethany until tomorrow, her excitement at the prospect was already infusing everything she did.

When had she ever been so giddy at the thought of spending time with a woman? And, more importantly, how had she denied herself this feeling for so long?

Because this felt great. More than great. And all the reasons she'd given herself over the years to avoid getting too close to someone, to avoid any potential hurt and rejection, seemed so hollow now. Spending time with Bethany, talking to her and making plans with her, gave Sarah a sense of satisfaction she'd never imagined. Was she still scared by it all? A little. But underneath the fear had always been a longing, a deep-seated need to be something else, and she was letting that need out now, and finding that it was more than okay to do so.

The brisk walk to her flat passed in a flash and minutes later she was out on her balcony, a glass of juice in her hand and a small cheese board on the table. She'd eaten a big lunch, so a snack in the warm evening air was all she needed. She smiled. Maybe tomorrow she'd invite Bethany back here after the exhibition; there was plenty of food in the fridge and they could make up an impromptu picnic out here on the balcony, maybe share a bottle of wine to celebrate the start of Bethany's holidays.

Already she could feel her clit responding to her thoughts and knew tonight would involve yet another indulgence in self-pleasuring. Every night this week she'd brought herself to orgasm, over and over, with fantasies of Bethany spinning through her mind. In the next moment, her brain very kindly replayed those fantasies and in the flush of eroticism that gripped her, Sarah let out a small moan and shifted in her seat. Good God, she was so wet again already. She laughed and shook her head.

Later.

Breathing out slowly, she reached for her food. As she picked at the cheese and sipped her juice, she idly flicked through Facebook on her mobile. This evening would be a lazy one, catching up on the world and maybe watching a movie on Netflix. And delving into her drawer of toys to see what she could use to bring herself the maximum pleasure later, of course.

Popping another piece of Stilton into her mouth and chewing contentedly, she startled as the phone in her hand began to ring and Bethany's name appeared in the caller ID.

Friday was a strange day. Now that the end of term was finally here, Bethany was relieved, of course. But she was also a little sad—her class this year had been, mostly, an enjoyable little bunch of urchins whom she had loved teaching. They had also worn her ragged, so her goodbyes were a tad enthusiastic as she looked forward to six weeks without them.

And undercutting it all was the antsy feeling she had woken up with and couldn't quite shake off. Her skin crawled with tension, goose bumps erupting without warning every time she allowed a thought about Sarah—and specifically her confession that Bethany got her wet—to enter her mind. Bethany was on edge, her entire body thrumming with something she couldn't name but which had certain parts of her anatomy begging to be allowed to do something about it.

When the last pupil left, and Bethany had pushed all of her possessions into two bags ready to take home, she let out a long sigh of relief. The walk home from the school only took her about twenty minutes; finding work so near to her flat had been a stroke of luck. Not only because it allowed her an opportunity to keep a little fitter, but also because it meant she didn't have to worry about Frannie letting her down as her aged engine threatened to die any day now.

As she bundled her way up the communal stairs to her first floor flat, she let her mind rid itself of the school day and instead fill itself with thoughts of the weekend ahead. Thoughts of Sarah.

Before she'd even shut the door behind her, Bethany was almost whimpering with need. As she dumped her stuff in an undignified heap on the floor by the sofa, she wondered what she could do about the heat raging through her veins.

There were two options.

One, she could bake, which always soothed her. But she didn't want a cake tin full of tempting treats around. Or two, make use of her trusty vibrator—again. It would certainly take the edge off things, but somehow a solo orgasm didn't appeal either.

She flopped down onto the sofa as a startling yet infinitely more appealing thought popped into her mind as option number three: have sex with Sarah. She could call her up, invite her over. Or just invite herself to Sarah's.

Nah, she couldn't do either of those things.

Could she?

She pushed herself off the sofa and paced the room, pulling at her T-shirt, which suddenly felt too tight against her heated skin. They already had a date planned for tomorrow, so she should just wait for that and see how things went. The fact that her libido was screaming that it couldn't wait a second longer was neither here nor there.

She snorted. *Yeah, right,* she thought, as yet more images of Sarah's beautiful face, her body, her laugh, and her husky voice, invaded Bethany's mind, as if working in cahoots with her libido to drive her out of her mind with desire.

Come on. Time to face up to what you want. Time to be who you want to be.

Carpe diem.

A plan started to form in her mind, and the more she latched onto it, the more impatient she got. Gripped with an almost feverish excitement, she practically jogged to her bedroom. After changing out of the clothes she'd worn to school, she jumped into the shower. The washing, shaving, and trimming—because she ought to be prepared, after all—was done in twenty minutes, but picking an outfit afterwards took an annoyingly long time. Finally, she settled on cropped black cotton trousers that she knew flattered her with a snug fit on her butt, and a cream top with capped sleeves and a plunging neckline that would show off her cleavage. Completing the outfit with the same strappy shoes from Saturday night—she'd noticed Sarah eyeing them appreciatively—she grabbed her handbag and headed out the door before she could talk herself out of it.

It was mad, she knew that—for all she knew, Sarah had suddenly changed her plans for the evening and instead of the quiet night in she'd mentioned on the phone the night before, was even now laughing and drinking in a bar somewhere. But Bethany was on a mission, and if it failed, so be it—at least she'd have attempted it rather than sit at home and wonder.

The Tube was still way too warm from the evening commute, and she was glad to transfer to the DLR at Bank, knowing that she'd be above ground soon and able to breathe fresh air. When Limehouse station came into view, her heartbeat sped up just as the train slowed down. She stepped off the train, walked down the steps, and found a quiet corner away from the rush of people exiting the station. Pulling out her phone, she sucked in two deep breaths before dialling Sarah's number.

"Bethany, hi."

Sarah sounded puzzled, and Bethany couldn't blame her. Oh God, was this an almighty mistake? Would Sarah freak out?

"Hi," she managed to squeak out.

"Hey, are you okay?"

Willing herself under control, Bethany swallowed before saying, "I'm fine. I've kind of done something a little crazy, and I'm hoping you're going to be okay about it."

"Okay," Sarah said slowly, dragging out the last syllable.

"I'm wondering if you can text me your address."

"Huh?"

"I'm at Limehouse station." Bethany waited for a reaction and when none was immediately forthcoming, she ploughed on. "I really want to see you, Sarah. I...*need* to see you. Need to touch you." The words came out in a ragged whisper as all of Bethany's pent-up desire swept through her body.

"Oh, God," Sarah breathed. "You're..."

"Crazy?" Bethany offered.

Sarah expelled a sharp laugh. "Yeah, but I was actually heading for wonderful. Amazing would have been in there too."

"You're not freaked out?"

"Nope, not at all. Just incredibly turned on."

Bethany moaned.

"Hang up and I'll text you my address."

CHAPTER 16

BETHANY SHOVED THE DOOR OPEN when Sarah buzzed her in, and strode over to the staircase that led up to her flat. Her heels clacked on the steps, beating out a rapid rhythm as she climbed as fast as she could. Every cell in her body was urging her onwards, faster, ever closer to the woman who waited for her just a few metres away.

She came to an abrupt stop at Sarah's front door and raised her hand to knock, but the door was pulled open before she made contact with the wood. Sarah stood in the open doorway, looking utterly delectable in three-quarter length blue yoga pants and a pale blue, sleeveless top. Bethany dragged her gaze up Sarah's body to her face, and they stared at each other for a moment, Sarah's eyes as wide as her own. Then, without a word, Sarah moved to one side, and Bethany walked into the flat. Her skin was tingling with anticipation, and as she turned to face Sarah who was slowly shutting the door behind them, every naughty thought she'd had since their first date hit her with full force.

She moved without thinking, but with purpose. Sarah gasped as Bethany pushed her back against the door, and the sound ignited a ball of fire in Bethany's belly. She leaned in and kissed Sarah, passionately, deeply. Pressing her body into Sarah, her hands grasping at Sarah's waist, Bethany poured all of her need for this stunning woman into every second of their kiss. Sarah's hands scrabbled for purchase on her hips, and when they finally got a grip, pulled Bethany in even closer. Sarah moaned, her fingers clenching and unclenching against Bethany's hips, her own desire obvious.

Pulling back to take a breath, Bethany gulped air and made to kiss Sarah again, but a frantic, whispered "Stop" had her eyes snapping open.

"What?" she asked in a hoarse whisper.

Sarah shook her head slowly. "I... You..." She swallowed and tried again. "I'm just...surprised. By...by this. Your strength. Your actions."

Sarah's face was beautifully flushed, her eyes dark with desire, and her breath came in gasping heaves, but Bethany had to be sure Sarah wanted this just as much as she did.

"If it's too much, I'll stop." She lifted a hand and rubbed a thumb gently across Sarah's lips, eliciting a satisfying moan. "But I told you I knew what I wanted, Sarah. It may have been a while, and I may not come across as experienced or confident. But you, here, now, like this"—her voice grew croaky—"is exactly where I want you. *How* I want you."

She swallowed, trying to ignore the shaking in her limbs as her nerves threatened to derail her from what she wanted to say. "If you need to be in control, then just say so, and we'll flip this around." She lowered her eyes for a moment, then gazed directly back into the depths of Sarah's. "But God, Sarah, I want you like this. Just like this. It's a need that is new to me, but feels so very, very right. There are things I want to do to you, ways I want to tease you, and unravel you."

At the small groan from Sarah, Bethany's confidence rocketed, and she straightened her spine and let her hands roam upwards from Sarah's waist towards her breasts. She stopped a centimetre or so underneath them, and smiled as Sarah pressed forward, trying to get her to move her hands higher. Nodding, feeling a rush so heady it almost took her breath away, Bethany whispered, "I want you at my mercy, Sarah. To do whatever I want to you, and have you desperate for more."

Sarah let out a strangled groan as her hands fluttered against Bethany's body. She tried to move again, perhaps to kiss her, but Bethany held her hands strong on Sarah's torso, keeping her pressed back against the door.

"Do you want this, Sarah?" Bethany asked, pretty sure she knew the answer but needing to hear it direct from Sarah's kiss-swollen lips. "Do you?"

Sarah was in a place she'd never been before with a woman: out of control. Bethany held all the cards. Her deceptive strength had Sarah pinned against the door. Her sultry words had caused a flood of wetness to soak her yoga pants and her heart rate to spike. She was completely at Bethany's mercy, just where Bethany wanted her.

And if she was honest, her fantasies always involved this, the one thing she had thought Bethany was least likely to do: dominating her. Something about Bethany's mix of shyness and nerves coupled with those bold statements she threw out had kept Sarah wondering just what Bethany would be like if her actions were as strong as her words. It hadn't really seemed plausible, but the fantasy had certainly done what Sarah needed it to do.

Fantasising about it was one thing, but was the reality too unsettling, too frightening to submit to? Her body ached for Bethany, literally *ached* to be touched by her, kissed by her, and anything else Bethany wanted to do to her. It was the last vestiges of her old persona that were holding her back.

Dominant-submissive sex was never about the physical, Sarah knew. It was all in the mind, in the power play, in the giving and taking of control. Sarah knew all of that, because that's what she'd always done with her previous sexual partners. Something about the fleeting nature of her trysts meant she'd never trusted anyone to see the side of her that screamed for release. She'd led and controlled every single one of those encounters, kept it to no more than one spice level above vanilla, and played emotionally safe.

Yet every time, Sarah had walked away with something empty inside her, something missing.

So, doing this now, with Bethany, would change her, she knew that for certain. She would leave behind the person she had been and embark on an entirely new sexual journey with this incredible woman who had appeared in her life as if by magic and swept her away.

Maybe she just needed a little more time to get used to the idea. Maybe if they just kept it more vanilla tonight, if Bethany let Sarah follow her tried and tested formula, then in the future they could see about Bethany taking up the role she so clearly wished to play.

At that thought, something seemed to sink in on itself inside Sarah. *You've wanted this for years*, it seemed to say. *And here it is, being presented to you on a plate by a woman who fires you up like no other has done, possibly in your whole life, and you want vanilla tonight? She's offering you double-*

chocolate pecan twist with white chocolate shavings and a cherry on top, and you're seriously standing here thinking about vanilla?

Sarah almost whimpered out loud as she felt her mind free itself of its shackles and doubts and fears.

"Yes," she whispered fiercely, staring into Bethany's eyes. "Yes, I want this. I'm yours. However you want me."

The release she felt at saying the words out loud was nearly palpable; she was surprised Bethany couldn't feel it too.

She expected a smile, or a kiss, or a groan—some obvious sign of Bethany's pleasure. But Bethany merely nodded, slowly, then ran her thumb over Sarah's lips once more.

"Good," she said softly. She licked her lips. "Now, I think we both know I'm pretty new at this, but one thing I've learned in reading up about it is the use of safe words. I think we should have one."

Sarah smiled, a wave of affection sweeping over her at Bethany's practicality, even in such a charged moment. "Okay, we can have one. But I really don't think I'm going to need it with you."

Bethany swallowed. "It would make me feel better."

"I understand. Marmite."

Raising one eyebrow in spectacular fashion, Bethany chuckled. "Marmite? Really?"

Sarah smiled. "It would stop you in your tracks, wouldn't it?"

"Yes, I suppose it would. Okay, Marmite it is."

She leaned forward and kissed Sarah then, the briefest touch of lips on lips, then without preamble, swept a hand up and over Sarah's right breast, cupping it, and squeezing hard.

Sarah groaned as her nipple responded instantly, hardening further than it was already and drilling into Bethany's palm through the fabric of her T-shirt. Sarah tried to push into Bethany's hand, to obtain more contact, but a quick "tut" from Bethany had her stilling her motion. Bethany was grinning, and Sarah smiled ruefully back.

"Patience." Bethany pressed her forefinger into Sarah's mouth. "Suck," she said, and that single word sent a throb that was almost painful through her clit.

Greedily pulling Bethany's finger into her mouth, she did as she was told and sucked and licked the digit as if her life depended on it. They locked gazes the whole time, and Sarah was thrilled to see Bethany's eyes darken to a grey-green that reminded her of wild storms over the sea. Bethany wasn't as calm and collected as she was portraying externally, and that brought Sarah even more pleasure.

Bethany slowly pulled her finger out of Sarah's mouth and stepped back.

"Where's your bedroom, Sarah?"

Her voice was husky with need and Sarah nearly melted into the floor. She couldn't find her voice, so merely pointed down the hallway and when Bethany stepped aside, walked past her, willing her hands not to reach out even though she longed for nothing more than to touch the beauty beside her. Bethany's heels were loud on the wooden floor as she walked behind Sarah, and each tap sent another shiver careering down Sarah's back. She fervently hoped Bethany would keep her shoes on; her legs and feet looked unbelievably sexy finished off in those straps and heels.

Sarah pushed open the bedroom door and walked into the room. The bed, metal-framed and simply covered in a white duvet, sat squarely in the centre of the far wall, with a pair of oak bedside tables flanking it. The wardrobe filled one corner, and the door to the en suite the other. Without thought, her gaze drifted to the bedside table on the left side of the bed, where she kept her extensive selection of toys, her harness, and all the accoutrements required to follow a safe-sex regime.

Bethany chuckled. "I assume that's where I will find everything I need?" she asked, coming alongside Sarah and running a firm hand down the middle of her back to cup her backside. Sarah shuddered and tried so hard not to lean into that touch, knowing Bethany would withdraw it if she did. How on earth had she misjudged Bethany so? This dominance was way beyond what Sarah had thought she was capable of, and it excited her in ways that left her knees weak.

"Yes," she whispered, not trusting herself to form more words than that.

"Good," Bethany murmured against her left ear, and the exquisite shivers that sound elicited sent another gush of wetness flooding between her legs. She was desperate for Bethany to do something about it, but at the same time willed the teasing to continue.

Bethany moved in front of her and sat, almost demurely, on the edge of the bed. Pushing her glasses up slightly with one finger—an action that was mystifyingly sexy to Sarah—she then crossed one leg over the other and leaned back, her palms flat against the bed. The movement pushed her chest upwards slightly, and her enticing cleavage opened up just a little further. Sarah sucked in a deep breath and waited.

Bethany's gaze roamed slowly over Sarah's body, starting at her face and working downwards. When it reached the apex of Sarah's thighs she clenched them tight; the thought of Bethany touching her there, or—preferably—licking, was mind-blowing.

"Undress." Bethany spoke quietly but somehow with more force than if she'd shouted.

Sarah quivered, and immediately set to work, slowly lifting her T-shirt over her head and smiling to herself behind the fabric as she heard Bethany emit what was almost certainly an involuntary moan as her breasts were revealed. Dropping the T-shirt on the floor, she dared to meet Bethany's gaze, and nearly choked at the unbridled desire she saw there. She dropped shaking hands to the waistband of her yoga pants and pushed them down her thighs. There was no underwear beneath. She blushed, knowing that her wetness was on full display now.

"Beautiful," Bethany murmured, and Sarah met her eyes. "You are stunning, Sarah."

The compliment caressed her.

"Thank you," she whispered.

"Lay down. On your back."

Sarah moved quickly, climbing onto the bed beside Bethany and lying as instructed. Bethany stared at Sarah's body, her focus clearly on the wet folds of Sarah's pussy.

"Open your legs, Sarah."

She spread them wide; there was no need for modesty. Bethany wanted her, and Sarah was more than prepared to give her everything that wanting entailed.

Bethany was nodding slowly as she stood and began to peel off her own clothes. She stared at Sarah's pussy as she removed each article, and Sarah burned with the need for more than looks. Bethany's gaze was nearly as arousing as a touch, and Sarah would never have known this kind of tease could affect her so. She watched, longing scorching her as Bethany's amazing body was revealed. Full breasts, pert and firm-looking. A beautiful curve from her waist to her hips, with a delicious little roll of belly just above her underwear. Her thighs were shapely and toned, and Sarah vaguely wondered if she worked out. Then all of her attention was drawn to the underwear Bethany was now removing: white, satin, and unbelievably sexy as it slid down over those glorious hips to drop to the floor at Bethany's feet. When her lover knelt beside her, Sarah's eyes nearly glazed over at the sight of Bethany, wearing nothing but a pair of gorgeous heels, perched on the edge of her bed.

Bethany had no idea how she was doing this. Yet it was real; Sarah was gorgeously naked, laid out before her, and hers to do with what she would. The range of possibilities that pushed themselves into her brain were dazzling, and she willed herself to slow down and sort them into some semblance of order. She was, after all, brand new at this domination thing—there was no point trying to run before she could walk. At the moment, making Sarah do as Bethany pleased was the thought that jumped into first place in the queue. Swiftly followed by teasing Sarah until she begged for release.

Reaching out, Bethany ran one hand down the length of Sarah's body, from her sternum to just above her pussy. Everywhere she touched twitched as she progressed, and she smiled; Sarah was already finding this difficult. Good.

She looked back up at Sarah, saw the aching need etched over her face and deep in her eyes.

"You truly want this, don't you?" she asked softly, as realisation dawned. "This isn't just about me, is it?"

Sarah shook her head, her cheeks pink. "Not just about you, no," she whispered hoarsely. "Taken me a long time to admit, though."

Her voice cracked as Bethany's hand trailed over her thighs, forefinger edging as close to her pussy as it could without actually touching.

"Bethany," Sarah groaned, lifting her hips, and Bethany pulled back, smiling, feeling devilish and loving it.

"No," she said softly. "Wait."

Sarah groaned again and flopped back down on the bed.

Taking a deep breath, knowing exactly what she wanted to do next, Bethany inched backwards off the bed and stood. Her own body was crying out for some attention, and she'd make Sarah give it to her, exactly how she'd fantasised.

The bedside cabinet had two drawers. Bethany pulled open the top one and was greeted by an impressive array of dildos, vibrators, and something else she couldn't identify. Like dildos but smaller and with a distinctly pointed shape.

She lifted one up, and asked, "What are these for?"

Sarah blushed even pinker—which Bethany found incongruous given the toys were in Sarah's own collection—before saying through a husky throat, "Butt plugs."

Bethany's eyes widened. *Wow.* Okay. Those would definitely see some action later. She put the plug back in the drawer and shut it, opening the second drawer immediately afterwards. This one contained a leather harness for the dildos, some pieces of silk that looked like they'd be very good for tying someone to the metal frame of the bed, a box of latex gloves, one of condoms, and a smaller box of dental dams. And an almost-full bottle of lube. That she could recognise each item was thanks to the website the sex shop ran; Bethany had availed herself of its illuminating tutorials on safe sex only last week. Smiling, she pulled out the silk, one pair of gloves, and a dental dam before closing the drawer and crawling back onto the bed alongside Sarah.

Sarah, who had been very well-behaved and not moved from the position Bethany had left her in, raised her head to see what Bethany held in her hands, then let out a tortured groan. Bethany smiled as she placed the gloves and dam on the bed, then ran the ribbons of silk through her fingers. They were a good length, and had fabric-covered D-rings at one end. Sarah was breathing heavily, her eyes wide and staring as Bethany's hands manipulated the silks over her fingers and back again. They felt deeply sensuous on Bethany's hands, but she couldn't wait to put them to use for their real purpose.

"Yes?" she asked, holding up the ribbons, her heart thumping crazily.

"God, *yes.*"

It took only a couple of minutes to firmly tie Sarah's wrists to the bedstead. With her arms spread wide, and her legs open, she looked wantonly sexy, and Bethany feared she might actually combust before they got anything started.

"Time to make me feel good," Bethany said, her voice wobbling slightly—not from lack of confidence, but purely from arousal.

"Yes," Sarah said, huskily. "Whatever you want."

Bethany shivered. She carefully lifted her right leg over Sarah and placed the knee on the left side of Sarah's head. Sarah realised where she was heading and moaned loudly as Bethany's left leg took up position on the other side of her head. Bethany felt daring, and exposed, and hugely turned on all at once as she grabbed the dental dam and held it in place over her own pussy.

"Lick me, Sarah," she said, hoarsely, bracing her thighs to support herself as she lowered down onto Sarah's mouth.

The first touch was exquisite, and Bethany nearly lost her balance as her entire body shuddered. Sarah's tongue was heavenly as it roamed over Bethany's swollen pussy, intensely pleasurable as it pushed inside her. Sarah seemed to be everywhere at once, her tongue flicking over every sensitive millimetre, driving Bethany mad with sensation.

"That's it," she said, her voice croaky with desire, "lick me hard. Good girl." She could hardly believe the words came from her mouth; it was liberating to fulfil this need that had blossomed in her.

Sarah's tongue moved faster. Bethany wanted to come and at the same time not—this felt too good to have it over too quickly. She pulled up slightly, and Sarah craned her neck to continue touching her.

"Not yet," Bethany panted. "But that's a very good start."

Sarah's lips were slightly swollen and damp from her exertions, her eyes as dark as coffee beans, her breathing ragged. "I...I want to make you come," she whispered.

"You will. Soon." Bethany sat back on her heels and pulled the dam away, ensuring she knew which side was up when she lay it on her thigh. Having Sarah pinned beneath her like this was giving her a rush she was sure would compare with a heroin fix, and her next move came as naturally to her as breathing. With her free hand, she slowly ran two fingers down either side of her clit and rubbed gently, agonisingly slowly. Sarah's eyes nearly rolled back in her head and she moaned, loud and long.

"Oh, God, Bethany. You're killing me. Please," she begged, staring intently at Bethany's fingers. "Please let me touch you. Lick you. Anything. *Please.*"

"Soon," Bethany croaked, her fingers increasing slightly in rhythm but still not directly touching her clit. "Just watch." She rocked her hips, opening herself up to Sarah's gaze, revelling in the agonised sounds Sarah made and the way her legs thrashed on the bed.

Hm, I'll need to tie those down too, next time.

At that thought, of Sarah completely tied up and open to her, Bethany quickly withdrew her fingers; she really was in danger of coming now, and she only wanted one person to make that happen.

She reached for a tissue from the box on the other bedside table, wiped her fingers carefully, then retrieved the dam from her thigh. Sarah whimpered as Bethany placed it back into position.

"Yes, Sarah," Bethany whispered forcefully. "Now."

Sarah arched up as Bethany lowered down, and her tongue slipped straight inside Bethany. A cry of sheer pleasure left Bethany's lips as she ground herself down onto Sarah's tongue, and when Sarah moved to lick firmly at her clit, she knew she was about to fall to pieces. Long, firm strokes had her grinding even harder, her breathing coming in short, hard gasps as her eyes shut tight and waves of sensation started in her toes and swept up her legs. The orgasm rushed through her, locking her thighs and arching her spine, her hands clenching the dam tight against her pussy as Sarah continued to lick her down from the initial spasms, through the rolling aftershocks.

She placed a hand on Sarah's head and pushed gently, letting her know she could cease her ministrations. Sarah looked triumphant, and Bethany couldn't blame her. That had been spectacular. She sat back on her heels again, her breathing gradually slowing, and smiled down at her lover. The view was slightly blurred—her glasses had slipped a little in the throes of her orgasm—until she eventually found the strength to raise a hand and push them up again.

"Very good," she murmured, and Sarah smiled widely.

"Thank you," Sarah said. "That was incredible. Please may I do it again?"

She grinned impishly, and Bethany chuckled.

"Soon. For now," she said, easing upright and lifting first one leg then the other away from Sarah so that she could sit on the bed beside her, "I need a little rest."

She dropped the dam over the side of the bed. Stretching out thighs and calves which were deliciously sore from straddling Sarah's head, she gazed at her lover's pussy, noting just how soaked it now was.

"But don't worry, I haven't forgotten you." There was a distinctly cheeky yet commanding tone to her own voice, and she liked it.

Sarah shook her head slightly. "Y-you're amazing at this," she whispered. "I'm in awe of you right now."

"Good," Bethany said, winking. "Let's keep it that way."

Sarah spluttered a laugh. "Can I kiss you?" she asked, as her laughter died down.

Bethany nodded, and shifted position so she was leaning half across Sarah's torso. Their lips met in a series of short, tender kisses that lengthened and grew more passionate as the minutes ticked by.

"You're incredible," Sarah murmured when their lips parted. Her eyes were wide, and she almost looked fearful. "I'm...I'm scared, Bethany," she blurted.

Bethany's heart clenched. "Scared of what?"

"Of losing this. Now that I've found it, found you, I...I don't want to lose it."

Bethany shifted again so she could stare directly down into Sarah's eyes. "I have no plans," she said firmly, "to go anywhere. I want this just as much, Sarah. Trust me." She willed Sarah to see the truth of the words in her eyes. This vulnerability was a little worrying, but she would do all she could to convince Sarah they were something worth keeping. "You're a beautiful person, Sarah, and I want you in my life."

Sarah's eyes shimmered, but she smiled, and let out a long sigh of what sounded like relief.

"Thank you," she whispered. "I'm sorry, I didn't mean to get so emotional, at this of all times, but—"

"Sarah," Bethany said gently, "there's no need to apologise. Not at all. This *was* very emotional—look at what we did together. Look how much you trusted me with that, and how much freedom you gave me to be who I really am. What we just shared was so much more than physical."

She could feel her own throat closing in at the emotion of the moment, and swallowed hard.

Sarah nodded, and her smile deepened. "It really was."

Bethany wasn't sure if it was too soon to break the seriousness of the moment, but she said it anyway. "And I think we ought to do some more of that sharing right now." She waggled her eyebrows as she reached for the gloves. "Open your legs, Sarah."

Sarah sucked in a breath but instantly did as she was told.

CHAPTER 17

SARAH STUMBLED INTO THE BATHROOM on Bambi legs. It was just before eight—it seemed she'd slept soundly, as she had no recollection of waking once she and Bethany had snuggled up after their exertions.

Catching sight of herself in the big bathroom mirror, Sarah stopped and stared. She looked…undone. Her hair was everywhere—being tied to a bed and thrashing about in the throes of pleasure would do that to a woman—and her face was flushed. Her eyes sparkled though, and even as she stared at herself, a smile tugged at her lips.

The previous night had left Sarah in a state of sexual euphoria she'd never experienced before. Her own pleasure had been intense, but more than that, it was knowing how much she had satisfied Bethany. Yes, she'd always been a considerate lover; of that there had never been a question. But what she and Bethany had shared had taken that to an entirely different level. Pleasing Bethany, obeying Bethany, giving Bethany everything she asked for had filled Sarah with a contentment, and happiness, and sexual satisfaction that she couldn't begin to put into words.

Unbidden, her fear of losing this—or worse, fucking it up—reared its ugly head again, and she had to clutch the sink as terror swamped her. Oh God, what was she doing? She was only going to get hurt. Or hurt Bethany.

I am not cut out for relationships, never have been. I should just end it now, before I get in way too deep, and—

Panic gripped her, and white noise cleared her brain of everything bar one thought: *I have to get out of here.*

She inched open the bathroom door. Bethany was still fast asleep, one arm thrown across the pillow above her head, the other reaching out to where Sarah's side of the duvet was pushed back.

God, she's so beautiful. Sarah stood and stared for a minute or so, and as she did, her panic receded a tad, at least to the point where she didn't want to sprint out of the flat.

Creeping across the bedroom, she retrieved her tatty old towelling robe from its hook on the back of the door and eased it onto her body. The door was thankfully silent as she pulled it open and left the room.

After pouring herself a glass of orange juice, she carefully slid open the big door that led to the deck and plopped herself down in one of the chairs near the railings.

Jonathan answered just before the call went to voicemail, sounding out of breath.

"Sarah? Bit early isn't it?"

"Sorry, did I wake you?"

"No, not at all, but I had to sprint out of the kitchen to get this."

"Ah, sorry."

"What's wrong? You sound...different."

She rubbed a hand over her face and sighed. "I think I'm having some sort of panic attack."

"What?" His voice went up a level. "Oh, God, are you okay?"

She rocked on her chair. "I don't know. I... Bethany spent the night. Last night. And this morning when I woke up and she was still there and still amazing and...everything, I just panicked." She swallowed hard. "I can't do it. I just can't."

"Do what?"

"This!" she exclaimed. "The whole relationship thing. If I walk away now I won't get hurt so much as when it ends later."

"Walk away? But... Why would it end?" Jonathan sounded mystified.

"I don't know," she ground out from between gritted teeth. Jonathan could be so infuriating sometimes. "I'll get bored. She'll get fed up with me. Someone else will steal her away—she's quite new at all this, remember, so I might not hold her interest for long."

Jonathan tutted. "Oh, Sarah. You could get run over by a bus tomorrow. Does that mean you won't get out of bed and live the day anyway?"

"Well, no, of course not."

Jonathan let out a small but triumphant cry. "Ah-ha! There you are then!"

"What?" Sarah was baffled. *How does that help?*

"Jonathan, in his own way, is trying to tell you to live for the moment, not waste your life doing the 'what ifs'." Evelyn spoke quietly. "And for once, I totally agree with him."

Her aunt must have picked up the second phone upstairs.

"How long have you been eavesdropping?" Sarah demanded.

"You agree with me?" Jonathan asked, his shock evident in his strangled tone.

Evelyn chuckled. "Do not get used to it, dear. It is not a habit I plan to nurture." She sighed. "Sarah, I was not eavesdropping. Well, not much. I did happen to hear Jonathan's voice and wondered who he was talking to, and then it became apparent it was you and so, well, I decided to join in."

Sarah shook her head. There was no point in having a go at her aunt. She meant well, as always.

"You really agree with him?" she asked, surprised at her aunt's apparent turnaround on the whole happy-ever-after concept.

Evelyn chuckled. "I do." She paused, then said, "Look how much you care, Sarah."

"Huh?"

"You care so much you're scared."

Sarah blinked. "I-I suppose so." She flicked her gaze out to the water as she let that soak in. "I'm scared in so many ways."

Evelyn's voice was gentle, and her words brought a lump to Sarah's throat. "What else are you scared of, Sarah?"

"I'd rather not go into details with you, but I'm trusting her with something I've never given anyone before," she said, her face flushing even though she had no audience. Jonathan's chuckle didn't help.

"Hm. I see," Evelyn said. "And why is this bad?" she asked, her tone firm.

Sarah gulped, and, not for the first time in her life, marvelled at the poise her aunt could display at even the most unsettling of moments. She pondered Evelyn's question, then drew in a deep breath.

"I'm scared that trust will get abused. Or she'll reject me, think there's something wrong with me, or something." The thought of Bethany doing any of those things writhed in her belly like the worst case of indigestion. Her voice grew small as she admitted the worst of her fears. "Or that she'll leave me, and I'll be hurting all over again, just like with Amber."

"I don't know who Amber is," Bethany said, and Sarah whirled round to see her in the doorway, her mouth dropping open. "But I don't plan on doing any of the things you just said." Her quiet voice carried a hint of hurt that cut through Sarah.

"Is that her?" Jonathan asked.

"Uh-huh. Gotta go. Bye." Sarah hung up without waiting for a response and put the phone on the table.

Bethany looked incredible. She'd found Sarah's other robe, the silky one that hung on the back of the bathroom door, and it fitted her perfectly, highlighting every delicious curve and showing off her shapely legs in the most alluring of ways.

"Are you okay?" she asked, tilting her head and looking confused. "I woke up and you weren't there, and then I heard you talking and…"

Sarah stood and slowly walked over to Bethany, who—thankfully—didn't back off.

"I'm…okay. Sort of." Bethany had clearly heard some of her conversation, so there was no point in trying to cover it up. "Shall we go in? I'll make us some breakfast, and we'll talk?" Bethany's face fell, and Sarah realised how that might sound. "Shit, no! I don't mean it like that. I'm not ending this." She stepped closer and ran a finger gently over Bethany's cheek. "Not if I can help it, anyway."

As she said the words, she recognised their fundamental truth, and something relaxed in her heart and her stomach. When Bethany smiled, that relaxation spread to her limbs and she returned the smile before dropping a soft kiss on Bethany's mouth.

"I do need to tell you what all that was about, though, I know that," she said, pointing at her phone.

"You do," Bethany said simply, before kissing her just as softly and then turning away to walk to the kitchen area.

Sarah followed her. "You sit there," she said, pulling out a stool at the breakfast bar, "and I'll rustle us up some eggs, okay?"

"Sounds good. I am rather hungry." Bethany grinned, but Sarah noticed a tightness around her eyes, and knew she'd need to talk to make that go away.

"I tell you what, let's hold off on the eggs for just a moment."

She grabbed a bottle of water from the fridge, then pulled out the stool alongside Bethany's, perching on its edge as she took a deep breath.

"Thank you for not leaving or being angry, or whatever," she said, trying to convey with her words as well as her earnest tone how grateful she was. She paused for a long moment to collect her thoughts. "I've spent my whole life, ever since finding out I was adopted, I guess, trying very hard not to put myself in a position where I would feel rejected. There's a rational part of me that knows that's silly—apart from Amber, no one has ever truly rejected me. But that rational part gets shouted down by the emotional part. It's the little girl in me who doesn't understand why her mother let her go, or why her parents were prepared to lie to her about her birth circumstances. And it's the teenager in me who lost her best friend just when she needed her most."

It was amazing how easily the words came, now that she was saying them. Yes, Evelyn—and lately, Jonathan—knew some of this, but Bethany was about to be the only one who knew it all.

"Amber was your best friend back then?" Bethany asked quietly, as if afraid to interrupt.

"Yes." Briefly she filled Bethany in on that particular story, then took a few sips of water before continuing. "After Amber's rejection, I convinced myself I didn't need anyone. I closed off my feelings, or at least I thought I did. I realise now I was deluding myself. Every time I had a drink, or six, or took a drunken one-night stand home, all I was doing was pretending not to care, and using drink and sex to numb the pain."

Bethany snuck out a hand and rubbed a thumb over the back of one of Sarah's hands. Her touch was warm, and soothing, and Sarah's throat tightened. She had to cough before continuing to speak.

"Before I knew it, I'd spiralled into a dangerous cycle, and was putting my career and my health at risk. Luckily for me, Evelyn has the eyes of a hawk, and she could see what was happening. At least as far as the drinking went. I think she hoped I would dig myself out of it, have some kind of epiphany or something. But when I didn't, she stepped in." She chuckled.

"She marched in one night, about eight years ago, and read me the riot act. There was no way I was going to argue with her either—deep down I knew I was in trouble. I guess I was just looking for someone to offer to help. And that was Evelyn." She shuddered. "I dread to think where I would have ended up if it hadn't been for her."

"She really cares about you," Bethany whispered, her thumb still making comforting circles on the back of Sarah's hand.

Sarah nodded, smiling. "She does. So," Sarah said on an exhalation, running her free hand through her hair, "that's where my mind has been all these years. And although I straightened up in terms of the drinking, and believe it or not, cut down on the one-night stands, I still wouldn't let myself feel. That was still way too scary. Jonathan's tried to push me to strive for something more, and Evelyn's told me to just do what I feel comfortable with. I think she was scared I'd revert back to the drinking and risky behaviour if I tried too hard to find that someone special and got rejected or hurt in some way."

Sarah turned Bethany's hand in her own and intertwined their fingers. "And then you came along." She met Bethany's gaze, noting how her eyes glistened. "And you turned all of that on its head. For the first time in my life—or at least the first time I allowed it—someone wormed their way under my shell and ripped my world open. Last night... God, last night was the pinnacle of that." She shrugged. "I don't know, maybe it was too soon or maybe it was perfect timing. Either way, surrendering to you like that, giving you the real me, who no one else has ever seen... It was incredible and terrifying all at the same time."

Bethany looked horrified.

"Oh, no!" Sarah said quickly, before Bethany could speak. "Don't get me wrong. I wanted it, I really did. It's just in the cold light of day, the fear of being hurt returned and I panicked. I mean, I literally panicked—I couldn't form a coherent thought other than to run away. And then..." She smiled at the memory. "I came back into the bedroom to get some clothes and there you were, asleep in my bed and you looked so bloody beautiful it literally stopped me in my tracks."

Bethany blushed as a slow smile crept to her lips.

"And that was enough to at least keep me here, in the flat. But I knew I needed to talk it out with someone, so I called my aunt's, and she and Jonathan were just talking me down from the ledge when you appeared."

"Well, I'm very glad they did." Bethany shuffled on her seat. "Do you really think I would do any of those things to you?"

Sarah vigorously shook her head. "No, I don't. Last night you were all the right things for me, and I know you wouldn't betray that. That was my fear talking, and we know my fear is very stupid."

Bethany smiled and reached out a hand to cup Sarah's cheek. "Yes. It is." She sighed. "I want you, Sarah. I want this, what we've started. In bed we're amazing, I think." She chuckled as Sarah nodded. "And I know we've hit a few bumps outside of the bedroom, but that picnic, and our dinner at Sheekey's, and the calls this week, they've all added up to something pretty special, and exciting, yes?"

"Oh, God, definitely."

Sarah inched off the stool and stood in front of Bethany. "I'm so glad we're talking like this. It takes me right out of my comfort zone, but I know it was what needed to be done. I'm sorry it didn't happen sooner. But I want you, Bethany, and I want us to be together and to see what we can make of this wonderful time we're having."

Bethany said nothing, but simply smiled, leaned forward and pressed her warm lips to Sarah's until she whimpered in relief, and elation, and pleasure. They kissed for who knew how long, but when they eventually came up for air they were both breathless.

Sarah was grinning, and didn't think she'd stop any time soon. Her hands rested on Bethany's hips as Bethany's fingers stroked her face, and played with her hair, and ran a slow trail down her neck to caress her collarbone.

"Can I ask one thing, though?" Bethany said, stilling her fingers. Her eyes narrowed, and a small frown marred her forehead above her glasses.

"Of course." Sarah braced herself, her heart pounding.

"Please keep talking to me. *Always*. I'm as new to this as you are, albeit for different reasons, and I have my own fears. I just think we have more of a chance at making this work if we actually talk, you know? I like you a lot, Sarah, and I already care about you, and about us, and about this magical thing that seems to be happening between us. So, please, if anything is worrying you, tell me. And I promise to do the same."

"I can promise that too." Sarah wrapped her arms around Bethany again. "I'm not used to it, but I'll make myself do it if it means I keep you in my life."

Bethany's frown disappeared, and her face blossomed into a smile. "Good." She hugged Sarah tightly. "So," she murmured, her lips close to Sarah's ear, "what do we do now?"

Sarah pulled back to gaze at her. "Start the day all over again and head back to bed? If that's too soon, or you're not in the mood—"

Bethany smirked. "Sarah, where you are concerned, I don't think you ever have to worry about me being in the mood."

Sarah flushed. "Well," she said, her voice huskier than anticipated, "that's good."

Bethany nodded slowly, tugging Sarah after her as she headed to the bedroom. "Yes, it is," she said over her shoulder, and the fire in her eyes set Sarah's clit throbbing.

Bethany eased her way up the length of Sarah's body, smiling to herself. Going down on Sarah, even through a dam, was rapidly becoming one of her favourites of all the things they had tried so far. Of course, they'd barely scratched the surface of what they could do to each other, and that thought sent a delicious shiver running right through her.

Sarah's breathing was heavy and erratic; her fingers still clenched the sheets, and she was shaking her head from side to side.

"That was..." Sarah murmured as Bethany laid herself fully on top of her.

"Uh-huh, it was."

Bethany leaned down and captured Sarah's lips in another blistering kiss. God, she could kiss Sarah all day long. Lying here on top of her, warm skin pressed together from chest to toes, everything seemed right in Bethany's world again.

"When I get my breath back, I'm going to do that to you in return," Sarah said, voice low and husky.

Bethany gazed into her beautiful brown eyes and smiled. "Mmm, yes please."

They kissed again, until the sound of Sarah's mobile ringing in the other room had them both raising their heads. Then Sarah's hands on the back of Bethany's neck pulled her back down.

"Ignore it," she murmured, trailing the tip of her tongue over Bethany's top lip before dipping into her mouth again.

The ringing phone stopped, then started again a few seconds later.

Sarah pulled back. "What the—"

"It's probably Jonathan, wondering what on earth is going on. Maybe you'd better answer it, put his mind to rest?"

Sighing, Sarah said, "Yep, I guess I had. Sorry."

She pecked Bethany lightly on the lips, then wriggled out from under her. Bethany rolled over and flopped onto her back, arms akimbo. She felt no need to cover her body—it was a warm morning, so the temperature in Sarah's bedroom was rather pleasant, and anyway, any doubts she'd had about being naked in front of someone again had been truly laid to rest hours ago.

Bethany couldn't make out Sarah's words, but her tone was cheerful and interspersed with laughter. She sat up to take a few sips of water from the glass beside the bed, and had just replaced it when Sarah bounced back in and launched herself onto her side of the bed.

"Wow, someone's perky!" Bethany said, chuckling.

"That was Evelyn, plus Jonathan chiming in somewhere in the background. They were desperate to know what happened after you appeared on the balcony. They are very happy to hear that we are back on track."

Bethany smiled. "Good!"

"I know. Jonathan also told me to tell you that he thinks you are a saint to put up with me."

Pulling Sarah into her arms, Bethany kissed the top of her head. "Nonsense. You're worth it."

"I am really glad you think that."

Sarah pulled back, wearing a serious expression, and Bethany reached out a finger to tap her on the nose.

"I really do. So don't worry."

"Okay. And you don't have to agree to this now if it's too soon, but they've invited us for a not-too-early breakfast tomorrow."

Bethany's heart leaped. Oh wow, Sarah really must be serious if she wanted Bethany to meet the most important person in her life.

Sarah seemed to take her momentary silence as reluctance. "Like I said, if it's too—"

Kissing her, Bethany smiled against her lips. "No," she said, as she pulled back, "I think that's a lovely idea."

"You do?" Sarah flushed and smiled. "That's…that's very cool." She blinked. "You do realise I've never taken anyone home to meet anyone from my family before?"

Bethany laughed. "Yes, I figured as much. Are you going to cope?" She softened her words with a smile.

Sarah feigned horror, her eyes going wide, but the grin gave her away. "I'll manage. I think."

"You will. They'll love me."

Bethany laughed, squirming as Sarah dug her fingers into her ribs.

"Wow, haven't we got cocky in the last twenty-four hours?" Sarah asked, grinning even wider.

"Ha ha, not really. But I am having fun playing like this."

"Yeah, me too." Sarah shook her head. "I feel like a whole different person with you. A better person."

"Aw," Bethany said softly, her emotions riding high. "That's a lovely thing to hear."

Sarah ducked her head and snuggled up against Bethany's chest.

"There is one thing though," Bethany said. "Sorry to get all practical, but I'll need to go home today, as I didn't exactly plan this through and I don't have clothes to change into." Bethany blushed, remembering her mad dash out of her own home the evening before.

Sarah looked up, a smile on her face. "Ah, yes, Miss Spontaneous. I was forgetting that in all the other drama I managed to conjure up." After a pause, she said, "Can I suggest we spend tonight at your place then? If you have other plans, that's fine, but I'd really like to spend the whole weekend with you, if we can?"

Bethany tapped a fingertip against her chin, pretending to ponder the question. Another dig at her ribs made her abandon the ruse as a laugh escaped her lips.

"Of course we can. I'd love that."

"Brilliant!" Sarah wriggled until she was more on top of Bethany than beside her. "Now, I most definitely have my breath back, so I think I need to make good on that promise, hm?"

She pulled a dental dam from the box by the bed and started moving down Bethany's body, planting soft kisses on any area of skin she passed.

"Oh, yes, you really do need to keep your promises," Bethany whispered, then arched her back as Sarah placed the dam in position and her tongue found Bethany's clit and began a gentle lapping. "Yes..."

CHAPTER 18

"YOUR FLAT IS SO CUTE," Sarah said, reaching for her tea and wrapping her free arm around Bethany.

They were snuggled up on the sofa, having both managed to find spots that were relatively lump free. Waking up next to Sarah in her own bed had given Bethany a wonderful sense of excitement and completeness. They were in a relationship now—a real, live relationship. She had a *girlfriend*. That thought alone made her want to squeal out loud.

"It's so much smaller than yours, but yes, I suppose cute is a good word for it."

"Oh, hey, it's lovely! You've decorated it beautifully. I can tell you've made the best use of the space you've got and it feels lovely here. Calm, and restful, and…homey. Sometimes I think my place is still a bit too stark, you know? Doesn't have a lot of warmth to it, because it's all modern and sleek."

Bethany nodded her understanding. "I don't think that, but I do think you could make it even warmer with just a few changes."

"Going to be my interior decorator as well as my girlfriend, huh?"

As she said the 'g' word, Sarah's eyes went wide, and her hand trembled on her tea mug.

Bethany chuckled, and patted Sarah's thigh. "Don't give yourself a heart attack. It's just a word."

"I know," Sarah said in a strangled voice, her eyes still wide. "I've just never said it before. Wow." She stared at Bethany. "It feels remarkably good," she said quietly, a small smile on her lips.

Bethany leaned in and kissed her. "It feels good to hear it," she murmured.

They finished their tea in silence, smiling at each other between sips, and kissing for a long time once they'd set down their cups.

"Ready?" Sarah asked.

Bethany inhaled and exhaled very slowly. "Yes. I think."

Sarah kissed her on the nose. "You'll be great. It's probably me we should worry about. Make sure you pack a defibrillator."

She grinned, and Bethany rolled her eyes.

The Sunday morning Tube was quiet. Thanks to weekend engineering works, they had to take a rather longer route, but they still arrived at Mile End in good time for Evelyn's ten a.m. invitation. It was another beautiful morning, and the short walk to the house allowed just enough time to feel the sun on their cheeks.

Bethany shuffled on the doorstep after Sarah had rung the bell.

"It's going to be fine. Like you said, they'll love you," Sarah said, slipping her warm hand into Bethany's and squeezing gently.

Her own eyes looked a little wild, though, and Bethany squeezed back. "And you'll be fine, too, okay?"

Sarah nodded, then turned as the door opened before them.

A handsome and groomed-to-perfection man met them with a wide smile on his face. He quickly greeted Sarah, then opened his arms to Bethany.

"It is lovely to meet you, Bethany," he said as he pulled her into a gentle embrace, kissing both of her cheeks. "I'm Jonathan, in case you hadn't guessed."

Bethany smiled, liking him instantly. "It's very nice to meet you, too."

"Come on in. Evelyn's in the garden, so go on through. I'm just topping up the pot and I'll bring the tea out in a sec."

"Thanks," Sarah said and, still clutching at Bethany's hand, led her down a grand hallway to a small room at the back of the house with double doors leading out to the courtyard garden.

It was a beautiful space which Bethany knew she would take more time to admire later, but first things first. The elderly lady Sarah led her to was sitting very upright in a high-backed rattan chair, a walking stick propped against its arm. She was smartly dressed, and everything she wore, from her clothes to her shoes and jewellery, spoke of money. But it wasn't intimidating or ostentatious—Evelyn simply looked as if she was born to it, like it was nothing more than a part of who she was. And she was smiling, which immediately relaxed Bethany.

"Evelyn," Sarah said, leaning down to kiss her aunt lightly on one cheek.

"Sarah, dear, lovely to see you."

Sarah sucked in a breath and beckoned Bethany closer. "Evelyn, I'd like you to meet Bethany, my girlfriend. Bethany, this is my aunt, Evelyn."

Evelyn's eyes widened just a tad at the word 'girlfriend' but her smile didn't waver.

"It's lovely to meet you," Bethany said, and smiled as Evelyn held out both arms.

They embraced briefly and gently; the scent of roses emanated from Evelyn, reminding Bethany of her gran, who had passed away some years before.

"Sit down, both of you," Evelyn said, motioning to the two chairs at right angles to hers.

They were arranged around a small, low outdoor table made of wrought iron with a glass top, and when Jonathan appeared moments later, he placed a tray with the tea makings on the surface.

Smiling, he poured out four cups and passed them round.

"She insisted on doing formal," he said, casting a withering look at Evelyn. "When it's just the two of us we drink out of old mugs like normal people do."

Evelyn huffed. "One does have standards when it comes to guests," she said, her tone biting. "Especially someone as important as this." She glared at Jonathan and smiled at Bethany, who tried very hard not to laugh.

Sarah smiled at her across the table.

"So," Jonathan said, "what did you two get up to yesterday after all the drama?"

The question was probably meant as innocent, but Bethany's cheeks flamed hot before she could do anything to stop them.

"Well," Evelyn said, peering at Bethany over the top of her cup, "I rather think that answers *that* question."

Bethany thought her face might actually melt from the heat her cheeks were generating.

"Evelyn!" Sarah shot the word at her aunt. "Really?"

Evelyn chuckled. "You know me, dear—far too old to shock."

"We spent the evening at Bethany's flat," Sarah said over Jonathan's sniggers. "She lives in Finchley in a beautiful first floor Victorian conversion."

"Oh, I do love Victorians," Jonathan said. "Any original features?"

Thankful for a far safer conversation topic, Bethany happily launched into a description of her flat, including the original fireplace in the living room, and from there the four of them moved onto an enthralling discussion that covered interior design, house prices, areas in London each of them knew, and how ridiculous the 'Gherkin' looked as an office building.

Jonathan put his empty cup down and rubbed his hands together. "Everyone hungry?"

"Starving," Evelyn said. "I was wondering how long you were going to keep us out here."

"Ignore her. She's always like this until her drugs kick in." Jonathan stood, winked at Bethany, and headed back inside the house.

"I do not, I hasten to point out, take *drugs*, as Jonathan so crassly put it," Evelyn said, shaking her head. "I do despair of that boy."

Sarah chuckled. "Firstly, he's a man, not a boy, Evelyn, and secondly, you adore him."

Picking at a piece of lint on the sleeve of her cardigan, Evelyn muttered, "Perhaps." She grabbed the head of her walking stick, and slowly eased herself up to a standing position.

"I will see you at the dining table," Evelyn said.

After her aunt was out of earshot, Sarah looked over at Bethany and smiled. "Did I warn you what it was like with these two?"

Bethany laughed. "No, but I think both of them are wonderful."

"They are." She walked over to Bethany's chair and leaned down to kiss her. "Let's go in, see if we can help Jonathan, yes?"

"Perfect."

They found him singing along to a radio in the kitchen while he beat a large bowl of eggs.

"Scrambled okay?" he asked as they walked in.

"Lovely," they said in unison, then grinned at each other.

Jonathan shook his head. "Oh, good Lord, they're already morphing."

"Piss off," Sarah said under her breath and Jonathan guffawed.

"Right, sausages are keeping warm in the oven along with the grilled tomatoes and mushrooms. I need someone on toast duty—Bethany, think you're up to the task?"

Bethany slapped her heels together, stood as straight as she could, and saluted. "Sir, yes sir!"

Jonathan rolled his eyes. "Oh, yes, you two are clearly perfect for each other." He grinned and pointed at the toaster, an uncut white loaf on a board in front of it. "Just get on with your job," he muttered.

Bethany chuckled, kissed Sarah, and walked over to her allotted workstation.

Jonathan tasked Sarah with laying the table, and the three of them hummed along to the radio while they worked. When Evelyn appeared, the click of her walking stick on the flagstones announcing her presence, her tut was so loud it was audible above the music.

"Must we have that racket on, especially on a Sunday morning?"

"Sorry, dear," Jonathan said, and immediately switched the station to classical.

"Oh, Beethoven," Bethany said, a smile instantly forming on her lips. "Symphony no. 6. Lovely."

All sound behind her ceased. She turned to find three pairs of eyes staring at her.

"You know your classical music," Evelyn said quietly.

Bethany blushed. "I...I do. My dad loved it and introduced me to it from an early age."

"I am a patron of the Wigmore Hall and regularly attend their lunchtime and evening concerts. Perhaps we could go together for certain performances?" Evelyn said, easing herself into a chair at the kitchen table.

Bethany stared. "R-really? Oh, Evelyn, that would be fantastic! Thank you. Thank you very much."

Evelyn nodded, smiling.

Bethany caught Sarah's eye and blushed at the look she found there—it was intense and tender, and she trembled at the power of it. They held each other's gaze for some moments, and only Jonathan's gentle clearing of his throat broke them out of it.

"Well," he said, his voice a croak, "I think we're about ready to dish up, if that toast is done?" He took his pan off the heat and tipped the scrambled eggs into a serving dish.

Bethany blinked and came back to herself. "Um, yes, I have four slices ready at least."

"That will get us started," Evelyn said. "If we wait any longer this will be lunch, not breakfast."

By the time they finished eating, Bethany's emotions were so high she knew she was in danger of crying. The interactions between Sarah, Jonathan, and Evelyn were a joy to watch—the love they all had for each other was clear to see. Equally, the tenderness with which both Jonathan and Evelyn—despite her sometimes gruff nature—questioned Bethany about herself and her life really touched her.

They retired to the garden for coffee after their meal. It was blissful outside—the warm sun bathed the courtyard in bright, golden light; sparrows flitted across the tops of the walls, chirping loudly and the wood pigeons perched in the treetops nearby cooed their repetitive call.

"This garden is amazing, Evelyn," Bethany observed.

"Thank you. It is my pride and joy. Well, after Sarah, of course."

Sarah blushed and her eyes glistened. "Thank you," she said, her hand shaking as she placed her coffee cup back down on the table in front of her.

"I am very happy to see *you* so happy," Evelyn said. She reached out a hand and Sarah took it.

Bethany could see the emotion on both their faces and sighed as Jonathan surreptitiously handed her a tissue.

"You too?" she said to him as she turned to nod her thanks.

"Always, whenever these two iron defences open up," he whispered, gesturing at Sarah and Evelyn, who were now simply holding hands and looking anywhere but at each other. "Gets me every time."

Bethany nodded. "I'm so glad she has Evelyn. And you."

"You care about her a great deal, don't you?"

She flushed. "I do. I know it's early and probably too soon but we just...connect, and we have done—more or less," she said, with a wry smile, "since I first plucked up the courage to call her and meet with her."

"She never did tell us where you two met."

She flushed all the way down to her chest. "Let's save that for another time."

Jonathan made to protest and she glared at him.

"Whoa," he said, holding his hands up. "Okay, Miss Feisty, I will withdraw. But I won't forget this is unanswered, madam."

He wagged a finger, and Bethany grinned.

She and Sarah left after coffee, but only after Evelyn had insisted on giving Bethany a slow tour of her beloved garden.

They took a cab back to Sarah's, having already agreed that Bethany would spend the night there before heading home in the morning when Sarah had to get up for work.

"Did you enjoy yourself?" Sarah asked as the cab pulled away after dropping them at the kerb outside her flat.

"Oh, Sarah, I had an amazing time! They are both so lovely, and watching you with them was really touching."

Sarah smiled. "Well, they *love* you, just like you said they would."

"And you seemed to be totally okay with how things went, yes?"

"I was! I still can't quite believe it, but yeah, nothing about that freaked me out. Amazing."

"Good. Because soon I'd like you to meet my mum, okay?"

Sarah whipped her head round. "Really?" she squeaked.

Bethany laughed. "Yes, really." She kissed Sarah. "You can do it. I know you can."

Sarah's smile was almost a grimace, and Bethany chuckled as she pulled her into a one-armed hug.

Sarah swivelled in her chair and gazed out of the window. There was no help for it, she just couldn't concentrate on her work today. Somehow she couldn't get the enormous grin off her face, nor could she shove away the images of Bethany that insisted on parading at the front of her mind's eye all the live long day. Bethany as she smiled. Bethany naked beneath her. Even better—Bethany above her, tying Sarah to the bed and commanding her to give Bethany everything she wanted...

She shook her head. This was nowhere she'd ever imagined she'd be, but now she was here, she couldn't imagine never having it. Bethany had literally turned her life upside down and it was the most fantastic thing that had ever happened to her.

As if conjured up by Sarah's thoughts, her mobile rang, and Bethany's name displayed on the caller ID.

"Hey, gorgeous," Sarah said upon answering, thankful that Roy was not in today and she could talk freely at her desk.

"Hi, how's your morning going?"

"I haven't got a thing done. For some reason, I can't seem to concentrate."

Bethany chuckled softly, filling Sarah with warmth. "I know what you mean. I'm supposed to be baking some bread to freeze for the Cornwall trip next week and I've got nowhere with that."

"It feels good, doesn't it?"

"Yes, it really does."

They were silent for a moment, then Bethany continued, "So, I sort of had this idea. And if it's too soon, it's okay, okay?"

"Uh-huh..." Sarah wondered what was coming next, but she had a pretty good idea.

"So, as you know, I'm off to Cornwall on Sunday morning, and I wondered if you might like to come to dinner at mine on Saturday night, and...meet my mum?"

Sarah swallowed, and although her heart rate picked up, she answered, "I think that's a great idea," and was proud when her voice only held the barest hint of a croak.

"Really?" Bethany sounded shocked.

"Yes," Sarah said, laughing, "really. If you can survive my two, I'm sure I can handle your mother."

"Well, that's...that's great!"

Realisation dawned. "You didn't think I'd agree, did you?"

Bethany chuckled. "Er, no, actually."

Sarah laughed louder. "Brilliant, I've outwitted you for once. I am chair dancing right now."

"Okay, okay, enjoy your little victory. I'm sure I can think of a way to pay you back." Bethany's voice had dropped that octave that made it husky, and sexy, and promised things that would make her scream with pleasure.

Sarah shivered and her eyes lost focus. "Oh, God, the minute you say stuff like that I become jelly."

"Hm, I do like to make you tremble, that's true."

"I am *so* not getting any work done now."

Bethany sighed. "Me neither. I may have just outfoxed myself."

Sarah sniggered. "Serves you right. So, are we still on for Covent Garden tonight? I will try very hard to get away by seven."

"That's fine. I'll have a mooch in the shops along Long Acre and you just text me when you're on your way."

"Deal. I...I can't wait to see you again." There were so many firsts for Sarah with Bethany, and every time she hit one, like saying those words just now, a thrill of excitement, not fear, ran through her.

"Me too," Bethany whispered. "Bye."

Sarah put her phone down on her desk and leaned back in her chair. She was buzzing. Being with Bethany was the best drug ever. Now she got what all the fuss was about, why Jonathan had lamented all these years over Sarah denying herself the chance for love.

Love?

She trembled. Yes, she supposed that was where she was heading.

Wow. Who'd have thought?

Her phone buzzed with a text message and she smiled as she read Jonathan's words.

> *I have the night off on Thursday. Drinks when you finish work?*
> *I might even go so far as to buy you dinner. Need to hear all the*
> *latest with your big romance :)*

She replied with a 'yes' in capital letters and put the phone back down on her desk. She really ought to get some work done now...

But someone whistling nearby caught her attention and she turned in her chair. It was Scott, and suddenly she knew how she could get the two men in her life to finally meet.

Well, this is new territory for you, Sarah Connolly—from one-night stands to matchmaker. She nearly laughed out loud.

"Hey, Scott!" she called before he could disappear.

He turned, grinned, and walked her way. "Hey, you. Tell me, are we still floating on cloud nine?"

Sarah laughed. "I think I'm at level thirty-two by now."

He rolled his eyes. "Yeah, yeah, rub it in why don't you."

"So," she continued, hoping her voice wouldn't betray her nervousness. "I was wondering if you were free on Thursday night? I'm going out for drinks with a friend and wondered if you'd like to join us."

He tilted his head. "A friend? This wouldn't happen to be your one and only gay friend, would it?"

Damn, he's good.

She raised her hands. "Okay, okay, you got me. But please, trust me on this. Jonathan is someone I have known for years and I love him to pieces. He's steady, romantic, very caring, and handsome. Not rich, but you can't have it all." When Scott took a half step back she stood and clasped her hands together. "Please, Scott, I'm doing this because I genuinely think you two have a lot in common. Just one drink, that's all I'm asking."

He looked away for a moment, then exhaled a long breath before raising his gaze to meet hers.

"All right. One drink." He shook his head. "Don't make me regret this, Connolly," he said, wagging a finger in her face.

"You won't," she said, smiling from ear to ear. "Trust me."

CHAPTER 19

"How did you get Jonathan to agree to that?" Bethany asked as she took the glass of wine Sarah handed her. "I thought he was against another work setup?"

Sarah grinned. "I cheated. I got Evelyn involved. You know what she's like—persistent is her middle name. She outwitted all of the arguments he had against it and he capitulated in record time. You know what, it's never occurred to me before now, but she would have made a *great* lawyer."

"I bet! So, have you heard from him since they went off to dinner together? Do you know if it went well?"

"Well, given how coy he was acting when I called earlier today, I'd say yes."

"Coy? Wouldn't he be shouting from the rooftops?"

Sarah shook her head. "No, when Jonathan is really keen on someone, he goes all shy, as if he doesn't want to jinx it somehow. I have very high hopes for him and Scott."

"Oh," Bethany said, her voice catching. "That's lovely. I don't like him being alone."

"Me neither. And neither does Evelyn." She chuckled. "God, watching her go to work on him about this was just awesome."

Bethany laughed and leaned across the sofa to kiss Sarah, who hummed with pleasure.

"So, my beautiful girlfriend…" Bethany gasped every time Sarah used that word, and she suspected she did it purely to elicit exactly that response. "We have a Friday night to ourselves. What, I wonder, are we going to do with it?"

Her wicked grin sent Bethany's temperature soaring. They hadn't seen each other since Monday due to various clashing commitments, and Bethany had been on fire all day at the thought of having a long Friday night into Saturday morning with her lover. Especially with a week apart coming up.

One thought in particular had set her blood sizzling. Sarah had asked her that first night they were together if using a dildo was something she'd want to try, and Bethany had shied away, too nervous of getting it wrong. She'd thought it would take some time to build up the confidence for it, but now, feeling Sarah's warm body snuggled against hers and remembering how hot Sarah had looked spread-eagled below her last weekend fired up her libido from nought to sixty in 1.5 seconds. The idea of pushing Sarah's legs apart again, then slipping inside her wearing a dildo, and fucking her slowly yet deeply, had Bethany's heart rate increasing and her breathing ragged.

"You okay?" Sarah murmured, looking concerned.

"Yes," Bethany breathed. She wanted to ask but didn't know how.

"You sure?"

"Yes. I…"

It was time for more of that dominance and boldness to come through. She set down her wine glass, her heart pounding and her clit throbbing. She took a deep breath and settled mentally into her role before taking Sarah's glass from her hand and placing it on the table next to her own. In a swift move that had Sarah gasping, she straddled Sarah's lap and brought their mouths close.

"Tonight I want to fuck you," she said, her voice clear and firm. "I want to strap on, pin you beneath me, and fuck you."

Sarah's long groan made Bethany's skin erupt in goose bumps.

"You'd like that, I take it?"

"Oh, fuck…yes…" Sarah hissed, her eyes wide and locked on Bethany's. "You…" She swallowed. "Please, Bethany, I want that so much."

Sarah's cheeks were pink, her breathing already ragged, and Bethany didn't want to wait another minute. Shimmying backwards, she stood and grabbed Sarah's hand, pulling her up to stand alongside her.

"Go to the bedroom. Strip and lay on the bed. Legs wide open." Her voice was husky with the desire that wrapped every inch of her body. Her pussy ached.

Sarah blinked, then moved. Bethany watched her walk—the sway of her hips, the tightness of her backside—and shivered.

Oh, yes.

She followed Sarah and watched from the doorway as Sarah obeyed her commands. As Sarah's naked body was revealed, inch by inch, Bethany's mouth became drier and drier. What a glorious sight that was.

Sarah lay on the bed and her gaze met Bethany's just as she spread her legs. Her pussy was already wet, that much was obvious even from across the room, and it took all of Bethany's strength not to sprint over. Instead she strolled, and smiled as Sarah whimpered in anticipation.

Her skin was prickling as she opened the top drawer of the bedside table. Once again Sarah's impressive collection of toys stared up at her. Focusing on the dildos, she let her fingers play over them as she tried to choose. They were all silicone, by the feel of them, and of various lengths, thicknesses, and colours. Knowing she was still a tad nervous about the act, she settled for a purple one that was about six inches long and only just over an inch wide at the base. Nothing too dramatic, but hopefully enough to satisfy.

Next she pulled a bottle of lube, a condom, and the harness out of the bottom drawer. This was the bit that had her most worried—how the heck did she put it on?

"Right," Bethany said, with more confidence than she felt. "I'll just be a minute." She walked as nonchalantly as she could towards the bathroom, giving Sarah a smile she hoped was seductive as she passed by.

Ensconced in the bathroom, she hastily removed her clothes and held up the harness once more.

Okay, so that has to be the front with the hole for the dildo itself. Four straps. Four? Oh, wait, yes. Okay, got it!

Quickly, she pushed the two straps that she'd figured out must go round her backside into their D-rings and tightened them. Then she did the same with the other two straps and stepped into the shape they made.

Okay, this works. Thank God.

She pushed the dildo through the hole that now sat snug against her trimmed pubic hair, and flushed with arousal as she manoeuvred it into place; looking down at herself with a dildo jutting out from her body, all she could think about was pushing it inside Sarah and fucking her.

And then she looked up, and her reflection in the large mirror nearly took her breath away. *Look at you, Bethany Keane. You look* good. *More than good.*

Sucking in a deep breath and willing her heart to slow just a little, she pulled open the bathroom door. Sarah was still on her back but her head was turned towards the bathroom, and her expression robbed Bethany of breath. Sarah looked ready, and willing, as if she would do anything Bethany asked of her right now. The sense of responsibility and power that gave Bethany was almost enough to bring her to her knees.

"You..." Sarah croaked, then cleared her throat and started again. "You look so fucking hot right now, Bethany."

Bethany nodded slowly and, drawing up straight, her body now flush with confidence at the effect she was having on Sarah, she pointed to the condom. "Roll that on for me."

Sarah scrambled across the bed to pick up the condom packet, ripping it open and discarding the wrapper haphazardly on the floor. Bethany walked over, keeping her gaze locked on Sarah's. When she was close enough, Sarah reached out with trembling hands and slowly rolled the condom into place.

It was one of the sexiest things Bethany had ever seen.

"On your back, Sarah," she said huskily, "I want to see you when I fuck you."

Sarah groaned and rolled back onto the bed to lay with her legs open. Bethany had researched this sexual act and knew that you could never have too much lubrication, so as she climbed onto the bed, she brought the bottle of lube with her.

"I'm going to go slow," she said, stroking down Sarah's body with one hand. "Because although I don't actually feel that nervous right now, I really want to do this right. Okay?"

Sarah nodded. "More than okay. I do like it hard and rough sometimes, but slow right now will be perfect."

She gasped as Bethany tweaked one of her nipples, rolling it and tugging it with her fingertips, then following that up with her mouth and teeth. It felt odd, having the dildo kind of bouncing between her legs as she bent forward, but it didn't actually get in the way of anything, so she ignored it. As it touched Sarah's belly, however, her lover gasped, and Bethany glanced up at her as she sucked on a hard nipple.

"Bethany," Sarah breathed, tortuously.

She pulled her mouth away from the delicious, fat nipple.

"Already?" she asked, smirking.

"Oh, God, yeah."

She also couldn't wait to feel what it would be like to be inside Sarah. She'd had her fingers deep inside her lover many times already, but she knew fucking her with a dildo would be an entirely different experience. So yes, this time, she'd let Sarah have her way. Next time, however... The thought made her smile as she shuffled backwards down the bed. She reached for the lube and squirted a generous dollop into her left hand. Finding Sarah's gaze again, she slowly applied it to the dildo, smiling as Sarah moaned loudly at the action.

Then, carefully, and with many small movements from side to side and back and forth, she positioned herself so that the head of the dildo was snuggled up against Sarah's entrance. Even that sight nearly blew her mind; Sarah's wide open legs, the waiting dildo, the tension in Bethany's own thighs as she momentarily held her position, all of it conspired to leave her shaking with desire.

"Baby, please." Sarah's voice was a ragged whisper, and the term of endearment—the first one Sarah had used, Bethany vaguely registered—caused a whimper to escape her own throat.

"Yes," she breathed, and moved just enough to push the head of the dildo an inch or so inside her lover.

Sarah moaned, and whimpered, and opened her legs wider as she brought her heels up to push against Bethany's backside.

"More," she begged, and Bethany obliged, unable to resist Sarah's pleas, unable to hold back from pushing deeper, needing to know what it would feel like to be buried within. She glanced down to watch the purple silicone disappearing inside Sarah's body, and her own pussy clenched in response. She'd fantasised about the act, but she could never have imagined what an effect it would have on both her mind *and* her body.

When she had carefully pushed all the way in, she paused, braced on her forearms, her gaze locked on Sarah, who was only just managing to keep her eyes open.

"Fuck me," Sarah said, firmly. "Fuck me, *please.*"

So Bethany did. Slow at first, making sure she understood how to keep a rhythm, how to balance herself and still be able to thrust in and out. But then faster, and slightly harder, as her burgeoning confidence and Sarah's breathy cries urged her on. Every now and then she glanced down to watch what she was doing, to feel as if she were starring in her own movie, watching herself from the outside as she fucked this beautiful woman. She was aware of the sounds in the room, and of the base of the dildo pressing tantalisingly close to her own clit, but her focus was on one thing, and one thing only: bringing Sarah as much pleasure as she could.

Sarah's hands were frantic on her back, her heels digging deeper into the soft cheeks of Bethany's backside. A slick sheen of perspiration formed between their chests; Bethany was now laying almost on top of Sarah, her hands clutching at Sarah's shoulders as she pumped her hips in an ever-increasing frenetic dance.

"Can you come from this alone?" Bethany managed to ask, her throat rasping with the effort.

"Not quite," Sarah panted.

"Then please, touch your clit. I want to hear you, Sarah. I want to feel you come with me inside you."

"*Oh, God.*"

Sarah slipped a hand from behind Bethany's back down between their bodies, and moments later Bethany could feel her rubbing hard at her clit, harder than Bethany had ever touched her there. She stored that bit of information away for future use, then concentrated on maintaining her rhythm and giving Sarah just that extra inch of room so that she could bring herself off.

It didn't take long—within a couple of minutes Sarah was jerking her hips, her free hand digging into Bethany's shoulder blade, her legs spasming as her orgasm ripped through her. She cried out, once, then held it for a moment, before the rest of the sound leaked out of her throat in fits and starts as Bethany continued to fuck her. Bethany's own heart was pounding; the closeness she felt to Sarah in this moment was making her eyes well up with unnameable emotions. She wanted to smother Sarah in kisses, hold her close, and never let her go.

Sarah's eyes snapped open, and she murmured, "Enough, thank you" and Bethany slowed immediately, making sure she didn't stop or pull out too quickly. She collapsed slightly on top of Sarah, her arms giving way, the dildo still nestled deep within Sarah but not moving now.

"Can I stay inside you, for a little while?" Bethany whispered, staring down at her. "Please?"

Sarah nodded, and kissed her, and kissed her again. "As long as you want," she said, kissing her way along Bethany's jaw. "As long as you want."

CHAPTER 20

THE SUN REFLECTED OFF THE window, obscuring the view of the shop inside. Still, Sarah was hyperaware of the products on display. She shuffled her feet and coughed but didn't move towards the door. In the window, she caught the reflection of Bethany's easy smile, as if she frequented sex-toy stores all the time.

Bethany smirked at her, and Sarah chuckled.

Look at her, standing there all cocky.

Not that she didn't have every right to be cocky—ten glorious months together had made sure of that. Bethany had changed. No longer the timid, yet forthright, woman Sarah had first approached in this very shop, now she was simply forthright, totally dominant in their bedroom, and Sarah loved it. She loved it especially because in the rest of their lives together they were perfectly balanced—it wasn't in Bethany's nature to try to dominate other than in the bedroom, but Sarah knew that in a way she did. She kept Sarah on the path—whenever she wobbled, and that was far less frequent these days, Bethany was there, stronger than Sarah would have imagined.

Her heart raced as she stared at her lover.

Thank God for this shop.

Thank God for that day when Bethany had come into her life. It was still early yet, but Sarah knew; this was *the one*. The woman she wanted to spend the rest of her life with. And next month in Paris, Bethany's favourite city, she hoped she'd get Bethany's agreement when she proposed on the banks of the Seine. The ring had been burning a hole in Sarah's pocket for a week now since she'd collected it from the jeweller's. If someone had said to her a year ago that she'd be happily planning to marry, she would have laughed them out of the room. But now, the thought thrilled her.

Bethany looked at her quizzically. "You okay?"

Sarah grinned. "Oh, yes," she said, strolling over to her. "Come on, what are we waiting for—I thought you promised me paddles?"

Bethany's cheeks flushed, and Sarah's pussy throbbed as wetness flooded her bikini briefs.

Dammit, another pair heading straight for the wash when we get home.

"Okay," Bethany squeaked, and Sarah smiled before dropping a soft kiss on her lips.

Bethany brushed her fingertips over Sarah's cheek, her gaze so full of love it made Sarah's stomach plummet as if she were on a rollercoaster.

Then Bethany turned and walked up the two steps into the shop, and Sarah followed, her hand at the base of Bethany's spine, her fingers tingling and her heart soaring.

ABOUT A.L. BROOKS

A.L. Brooks currently resides in London, although over the years she has lived in places as far afield as Aberdeen and Australia. She works 9–5 in corporate financial systems and spends many a lunchtime in the gym attempting to achieve some semblance of those firm abs she likes to write about so much. And then promptly negates all that with a couple of glasses of red wine and half a slab of dark chocolate in the evenings. When not writing she likes doing a bit of Latin dancing, cooking, travelling both at home and abroad, reading lots of other writers' lesfic, and listening to mellow jazz.

CONNECT WITH A.L. BROOKS
Website: albrookswriter.com
E-Mail: albrookswriter@gmail.com

OTHER BOOKS FROM YLVA PUBLISHING

www.ylva-publishing.com

UP ON THE ROOF
A.L. Brooks

ISBN: 978-3-95533-988-3
Length: 245 pages (88,000 words)

When a storm wreaks havoc on bookish Lena's well-ordered world, her laid-back new neighbor, Megan, offers her a room. The trouble is they've been clashing since the day they met. How can they now live under the same roof? Making it worse is the inexplicable pull between them that seems hard to resist. A fun, awkward, and sweet British romance about the power of opposites attracting.

A WORK IN PROGRESS
(The Window Shopping Collection)

L.T. Smith

ISBN: 978-3-95533-850-3
Length: 121 pages (37,000 words)

Writer Brynn is in love with her best friend and muse, Gillian. The problem is Gillian is straight. And she's more focused on enlisting Brynn to see whether her fiancé is a cheat.

This UK rom-com, part of the Window Shopping Collection, proves that the path to true love has a few bumps in it.

One Way or Another
© 2018 by A.L. Brooks

ISBN: 978-3-96324-094-2

Also available as e-book.

Published by Ylva Publishing, legal entity of Ylva Verlag, e.Kfr.

Ylva Verlag, e.Kfr.
Owner: Astrid Ohletz
Am Kirschgarten 2
65830 Kriftel
Germany

www.ylva-publishing.com

First edition: 2018

Credits
Edited by Alissa McGowan and Sheena Billet
Cover Design and Print Layout by Streetlight Graphics

CPSIA information can be obtained
at www.ICGtesting.com
Printed in the USA
FFHW02n0809091018
48745784-52817FF